Forever 🌹 *Romances*

MORE THAN A SUMMER'S LOVE

Yvonne Lehman

Forever ❦ Romances

is an imprint of
Guideposts Associates, Inc.
Carmel, NY 10512

Dedicated to my American daughter Cindy, and our sponsored Cindy, in the Philippines

I could not love thee, dear, so much,
Loved I not honor more.
— Richard Lovelace

CHAPTER 1

WHAT AN INCREDIBLY HANDSOME MAN, Stacey thought, spotting a naval officer clad in crisp whites in the waiting room of the Manila International Airport. Directly ahead of her, a young Filipino, also in military uniform, came to attention and saluted smartly. The handsome officer returned the salute. As his hand dropped to his side, his eyes swept Stacey, and he gave her a dazzling smile.

She smiled back, not caring whether he thought she might be flirting. After all, she just might be. And he *had* smiled first. Stacey felt a surge of joy. Shimmering sunshine was just beginning to melt away the chill of the morning. Her first day in the tropical nation of the Republic of the Philippines promised to be a spectacular one.

Just as she shifted her gaze to search for Maila, who was supposed to be meeting her, she heard her name.

"Stacey Stamford."

In one swift movement the officer had removed his cap with the scrambled-eggs insignia and was extending a hand toward her.

Stacey's knees bent slightly as she set down her overnight case and balanced the strap of her heavy bag more securely over one shoulder. Straightening, she placed her hand in his. His grip was warm and firm. He did not release it immediately.

"Do I know you?" she asked, her brown eyes studying his face intently. Quite sure she had never been acquainted with anyone like him, her mind quickly scanned the pages of memory, trying to imagine what young boy from her past could have grown into such an excellent specimen of masculinity. There was an air of maturity in the finely chiseled features—straight nose, full lips, strong jaw line.

Long dark lashes framed blue eyes, accented by heavy brows the color of his rich brown wavy hair. But now, he smiled again, and the lips spread, dimpling his cheeks with boyish appeal. The permanent creases at the corners of his eyes deepened as he introduced himself.

"I'm Eric Farrington," he said, as if she should have known.

"Mr . . . I mean, Commander . . ." Stacey began, feeling the life returning to her hand that was growing warm in his.

"Eric," he insisted, inclining his head slightly, and dimpled again. "Maila might have mentioned me."

"Only the name," Stacey replied, and a single sentence that had seemed rather insignificant now burned in her brain. Several years ago Maila had written that a Commander Farrington had been especially helpful to her family. Then, two years ago she wrote: "Now that I've graduated from nurses' training, Commander Farrington insists that I call him Eric."

How fortunate to have such an interested benefactor, Stacey had thought when she read those words. Now, seeing Eric Farrington for herself, she was reminded of her initial impression. *Yes, how very fortunate for Maila*.

"Where is Maila?" Stacey asked, her eyes darting around the airport searching for the young woman with whom she had corresponded for the past ten years, since they were both fourteen years old.

Eric released her hand at last. His dimples vanished, leaving behind smoothly tanned cheeks, with only a slight crease at each side of his mouth. His countenance grew more serious and his deep voice was edged with concern. "There was an emergency at the hospital last night. Maila was called in early this morning for extra duty and asked me to meet you. Sorry to disappoint you."

"Oh, I'm not disappointed," Stacey assured him hastily, then rather than cover her blunder with something equally awkward, bent to retrieve her overnight case.

"Shall we get the rest of your luggage?"

"I *would* like to freshen up a bit—" then seeing Eric lift his cuff to glance at his watch, she added, "if there's time."

"We'll take time," Eric replied, exposing his dimples again. "The freshen-up room is right over there." He nodded toward a door. "Give me your baggage tickets and you can join me in a little while."

"Thank you. I'll do that." Stacey swung her shoulder bag around and dug into it for her ticket holder. Finding her baggage checks, she handed them to Eric.

"You need that?" he asked, pointing to the overnight case.

"No." Stacey laughed. "My face is in *here*. " She patted her shoulder bag.

"Then you should thank whomever loaned you theirs," he remarked on a perfectly serious note, "for it is very beautiful—much more so than in your photos."

While Stacey groped for a suitable denial, he took the overnight case from her, turned and began striding across the lobby. "I'll meet you at the baggage carousel," he called over his shoulder. " Just follow that sign."

Amazing, Stacey mused a moment later, looking into the mirror in the restroom, *how a compliment from an attractive man can set a girl's eyes to sparkling and bring a glow to her cheeks. Even when it's a compliment from a man who just might belong to her pen pal of ten years.*

Grateful for the blunt cut of her tawny hair, she brushed it straight back to her shoulders, pulled a few short strands across her forehead into bangs, and tucked several long tresses behind one ear, exposing a large, rectangular-shaped gold earring, matching the watch she wore on a gold chain around her neck. After applying a bronze gloss to her lips, Stacey gave a final appraisal to her bone-colored, tailored suit, complete with pumps that matched a rust-colored silk blouse, and felt she might fool anyone into believing she was a level-headed, sensible young woman on an important summer mission.

"I can't believe my luggage really made it!" Stacey exclaimed, walking up behind Eric. She had already taken note of the muscles rippling in his forearms with the exertion of lifting her bags from the carousel.

"Sounds like an experienced traveler," he remarked, turning to face her.

"Not really." Stacey confessed. "The extent of my flying has been pretty limited—once to visit an aunt in California, and another time to visit a foster family of one of my foreign students in Florida. It's really from the students that I've learned luggage occasionally doesn't arrive with the person, and sometimes it's even tossed out over the Pacific, or ends up in some remote place like Switzerland!"

After a moment of shared laughter, he asked, "You like your work very much, don't you, Stacey?"

"Being a Career & Guidance Counselor at a small college may not sound very exciting to you, but it has been a life-changing experience for me. I'm just so thrilled at the prospect of doing my field work here in the Philippines, especially since it will give me an opportunity to get to know Maila better." She cocked her head. "Here I am, all set to adapt to another culture, and who is the first person I meet—another American!" she exclaimed with mock exasperation. "You are American, aren't you, Eric?"

"From all over the country," he said, then explained. "I was a military brat, and the longest period of time I ever spent in one spot, before coming to the Philippines, was at Annapolis. Oops," he interrupted, "I'd better signal that skycap . . ."

"You see," he turned toward her again. "I have looked forward to this for a long time. For many years now I've wanted to thank you personally for what you've done for Maila."

She blushed beneath his intense look before he turned to speak to the skycap, then led the way toward a side exit.

Outside, bathed in warm sunshine, Stacey watched as Eric's eyes skimmed the brilliant blue sky with it's fluffy white clouds. He smiled down at her. She knew he appreciated the beauty of the morning as much as she.

"Here we are," he said, stopping beside a royal blue Lincoln and unlocking the trunk. While the skycap, who had followed closely behind with the cart was stowing the luggage inside, Stacey rummaged in her shoulder bag. When she found her billfold and looked up, she saw that Eric had already taken a bill from his wallet.

"Want to put your bag in here?" Eric asked with dancing eyes.

Stacey flashed him a grateful smile and handed him her shoulder bag. Waving off the skycap, Eric unlocked the passenger door and handed her into the car. After sliding behind the wheel, he leaned toward her. Feeling the force of his gaze, she turned to encounter a pair of electric blue eyes. She was amazed to see what the light blue interior did to them, lending a magnetism that left her breathless.

"Stacey," he said quietly, and reached for her hand, holding it in his palm, while he draped the other arm casually over the steering wheel. "Thank you for being here. For what you've done for Maila. For what you've done for me."

Stacey glanced down at his broad chest where the white coat of his uniform was pulled taut. Embarrassed by the path her eyes had taken, she blinked and shook her head.

"It was so little," she protested. Her monthly sponsorship of Maila had, indeed, seemed small compared to her own income, for she knew she wasted more than she mailed to the Philippines once a month.

"One of the mottos of the Children's Fund is that a little works miracles. And Stacey, maybe your sponsorship was little by American standards, but here— for Maila—it was a miracle. It was because of you, Stacey, that I came to know her. It was because of you . . . ah," he sighed deeply and his expression lost its intensity. "Forgive me. I seem to be blurting out everything at once—all the the things I've longed to say to you. You've only just arrived. I must be patient."

With that, he squeezed her hand, then released it and proceeded to start the engine. Stacey gazed beyond the windshield. She had known this intriguing man for less than an hour, yet she would never forget the color of his eyes. They were the same pure hue as the early morning sky over Manila.

During the smooth ride, she scanned the landscape as Eric pointed out places of interest. Lush green shade trees lined the wide boulevards, and the blue-green waters of Manila Bay sparkled as the sun danced upon its surface. Fishing vessels moved slowly toward distant islands, surrounded by tall mountain peaks.

Excitement churned in Stacey as she heard Eric describe the islands as "the Pearl of the Orient." Interesting places and historical facts had always fascinated her, but not so much as people. She turned slightly in the seat, crossed her shapely legs, and smoothed her skirt. One shoulder rested against the back of the seat, as if she had found a landmark infinitely more appealing than the vistas that stretched out before them.

Observing Eric's strong profile, Stacey longed to know more about the man than the tour-guide façade he was presenting.

Eric glanced at her and smiled before returning his eyes to the road. "And how are your parents?" he asked in a more relaxed tone, as if sensing her mood.

"They're fine," she began with a standard reply. "They're delighted about my trip and feel it's a wonderful opportunity. However," she shook her head, remembering the events of the past few weeks, "they've forced me to read every article that's been written about the political and social unrest in the Philippines. While their attitude is understandable, their warnings strongly resemble those I rebelled against during my teen years."

Seeing her smile, Eric concluded, "Apparently you don't resent them now."

"Not at all," she replied warmly. "I appreciate my parents more every day."

"Fortunately, that's a part of the maturing process," he said, watching the road while maneuvering the car around a curve. "And the most unexpected events can prove to be the most important catalyst for growth—like the accident that put your father out of work."

"Accident?"

"When you were fourteen," he explained with a tilt to his lips.

Immediately Stacey's thoughts were thrust backward to the time when her father had broken both legs in an automobile accident. When one of the bones failed to knit properly, his return to teaching at the university had been indefinitely postponed. Her mother had been forced to take a secretarial position, leaving Stacey with more home responsibilities.

'My sense of security was shaken for a while," Stacey admitted, "but—you're right—it marked a milestone in my life. Dad, whom I had considered indomitable, was suddenly helpless. And he needed me." Her voice softened. "Difficulties really can bring people closer together."

She looked quickly at Eric, wondering if he thought her sloppily sentimental.

But he was nodding in agreement. "They teach us valuable lessons we don't forget."

Then the impact of the conversation struck her. She had never seen Eric Farrington before today, yet she was sharing some of her deepest feelings with him. "How did you know about my father? And his accident?"

"That's when I became aware of the relationship between you and Maila," he replied, glancing her way. "The entire Children's Fund Center was greatly impressed with the fact that you were sending your baby-sitting and odd-job earnings for Maila's support when your parents felt they could no longer obligate themselves."

"But that was such a small gesture."

"Not for a fourteen-year-old girl, Stacey," Eric insisted, admiration in his voice. "Especially one with your family difficulties. At the time John Carlson told me about it, *my* main concern was whether or not Ingrid would marry me. But you gave me something else to consider. If a young girl could care about the people here halfway across the world, surely I could do something to alleviate the poverty I was seeing first-hand. It was the beginning of a new direction for my life, Stacey."

Dropping her eyes under his approving glance, Stacey idly traced a pattern along the hem of her skirt with her finger. After a thoughtful pause, she asked, "And . . . did you marry Ingrid?"

A heavy silence hung in the air. Unaccountably Stacey felt the pulsing vibration of her heart. If he were married, that was that. If he were not, he would certainly belong to someone by now. Perhaps to Maila.

Finally, he spoke. "No, Ingrid and I did not marry. Not each other, anyway."

"You . . married someone else?" she asked faintly.

"No. She married her high-school sweetheart. But I was twenty-four then, Stacey. And I wonder if what I went through is what you are experiencing now."

That remark caught her totally off guard. "I-I?" Stacey stammered, astounded. "What . . .?"

"With Randy," he explained sympathetically.

"Randy? What . . . how do you know about that?" A sense of indignation rose in her. "I thought my correspondence was confidential, but you seem to know all about my parents. About . . . Randy." She took a deep breath.

"I also know how hot-headed you can be, and I'm getting scared," Eric replied in mock trepidation, eying her warily.

Even her occasional flare-ups of temper were

15

known to him. "We've been together less than an hour and already I'm yelling at you," she said apologetically.

He grinned. "Our first argument."

Stacey had to confess her curiosity to know more about him, but balked when he or anyone else probed too deeply into her own life. Feelings she had tried to put behind her were now as near the surface as the color she knew had risen to her face when Eric mentioned Randy.

Watching his solemn profile, Stacey felt he was waiting for her to make a decision. She could talk about some of the landmarks they were passing. She had read enough history to formulate some intelligent questions about Manila. She could ask his feelings on the political and social situation in the Philippines. He would undoubtedly smile, answer politely, and they would engage in enlightening, surface conversation.

Yet he had given her an opening, an invitation, for complete honesty. Anything less, she felt, would sever this strange bond that had begun to form between them. With a slightly quavering voice, she began, "I'm sorry. I was just surprised you knew about such a personal matter. And it still hurts to talk about it, I guess."

Eric nodded. "That's what I feared. You're going through a rough time. And who does a counselor have to confide in?" He reached over and covered her hand with his. "Perhaps here in the Philippines you can bare your soul to a friend, namely Eric Farrington. I have broad shoulders," he offered.

So she had noticed. "Thanks," she said softly.

He squeezed her hand and returned his to the wheel. She looked at her hand still tingling from his touch. He had intended it to be a comforting gesture; she should not be remembering its masculine strength.

His voice was a welcomed intrusion on her

thoughts. "Did you ever share any of Maila's letters with anyone, Stacey?"

She looked up. "With anyone? Everyone!" she admitted, then caught his point. She smiled ruefully.

"You see, Stacey," he began to explain, "that one incident when you were fourteen was shared with me because John is a friend of mine. In a way it was a reprimand for my own self-centeredness. But he doesn't betray confidences. Neither does Maila. Through the years, when I asked about you, she would give me a running account. You were the most exciting person in her life."

Stacey smiled at that and Eric continued. "She told me about your sixteenth birthday party, your campaign for president of student council, high school graduation, the night you spilled punch on your new formal when the best-looking guy in school asked you to dance at the Senior Prom."

"It wasn't funny then, though," she said.

"And she told me about the time you ran into a chair and broke your toe."

"Ouch! I can still feel it." She grimaced.

His dimple appeared, then disappeared as he added, "Maila also casually mentioned when you began dating Randy. You wrote that you would probably marry him. Then you broke it off. It was off and on for a while. Maila felt your unhappiness very keenly, Stacey. But she didn't give me any details about your relationship with him," he assured her. "Only sketchy information."

"I didn't tell her the reasons," Stacey said. "Neither of us were that personal in our letters. But I suppose you can learn a lot about people just from the surface remarks they make."

'That's true," Eric replied. "So I hope you will forgive me if I seem too personal too quickly. To you I may be a stranger. But Stacey, I feel that I've known you for ten years."

17

A quick laugh escaped her throat before she said coyly, "But I do feel at a decided disadvantage. My life history is known to you, but I know so little about yours."

She expected dimples, but he spoke seriously. "You're right, Stacey. It isn't fair. So I'm going to give you every opportunity to know me. You'll see so much of me you'll probably scream 'uncle' and run to the nearest aid station."

"I doubt that," Stacey replied and felt her response was not the expected one. She should have laughed at his pretended seriousness, or agreed with him. One certainly shouldn't reveal she has fallen under a stranger's spell in so short a time. Seeing a slight question form in his eyes and a little muscle tug at his lower lip, Stacey decided to add, "Any friend of Maila's should be a friend of mine."

"My sentiments exactly," he said with a warm smile. "That's one reason I insisted upon meeting you at the airport."

And what were the other reasons, she wondered. Was he trying to tell her he and Maila were more than friends? Then the phrase Maila had written again tugged at her mind, "He insists that I call him Eric."

"Beneath us is the Pasig River," Eric was saying now and Stacey realized they were crossing a bridge. "Then we're on our way to downtown Manila."

Soon they were bombarded with traffic and the fast-moving vehicles Eric called jeepneys. "They used to be military jeeps, but have been converted to public transportation use, carrying eight to ten passengers," he explained.

"Colorful," Stacey observed, seeing the many signs and pictures painted on the bodies of the jeepneys.

"And noisy," Eric added. Loud music with a distinct western sound drifted in through the closed windows of the Lincoln.

The Americanization of Manila was obvious in its tall buildings of steel, glass and concrete. Neon signs flashed American brand names. People walked the streets in westernized clothing. The scene was much like that in any American city, with the exception of the vast numbers of persons on the sidewalks, in the jeepneys and buses.

Upon closer speculation, however, she noted ancient buildings among the new. They drove past an old colonial church with grilled windows and walled gardens, exemplifying the Spanish influence of days gone by. Glimpses of stone and rubble spoke of wartime, foreign and civil.

Eric pointed out the hospital where Maila was at work. A few blocks further he turned into a narrow street. Here on each side were rows of cream-colored stucco apartment buildings, some in grave disrepair.

Eric pulled to the curb and stopped. Passers-by glanced their way and continued walking.

"Why are we stopping here?" Stacey asked.

He looked at her from eyes shaded by the brim of his cap. "This is Maila's apartment," he said taking the keys from the ignition.

Stacey turned in her seat to peer through the car window at the stucco flat that rose several stories into the sky. Opening the door, she got out, still surveying the building, while Eric set her bags on the sidewalk.

"Three flights up and no elevator," he said. "Let's set these inside the foyer."

Inside Stacey eyed the stairway skeptically. "Up there?" she asked.

"Yes, and I have a bad leg," Eric replied. For a moment she thought him serious. Then the dimples dented his cheeks.

Stacey laughed. "Surely you are an officer . . . and a gentleman."

"I shall work on the latter," he said, picking up the two heavier bags. "Follow me."

Stacey followed with her shoulder bag, the overnight case and a lighter bag. They stopped at the second landing and leaned against the drab gray wall to rest.

"You all right?" he asked.

Stacey nodded. "I must say, my aerobics and light weight-lifting have finally paid off. I always told myself, 'Stacey, someday you'll carry luggage up three flights of stairs in the Philippines.'"

"It does make a difference," Eric said.

Conscious of his lean muscular frame, Stacey felt herself coloring again.

When they arrived at the third floor, Eric stopped in front of the first door on the left. She watched silently as he unlocked the door of Maila's apartment, then returned the key to his pocket. Then he set the bags at one side of the room. Eric closed the door.

"Like some coffee?" he asked.

"I'd love some," she replied gratefully.

He headed for the far end of the room, opposite the entrance, past a kitchen table, made a left and disappeared.

Dim light invaded the living room from an open doorway on the left as it spread across the stark walls, emphasizing the scant furnishings—a brown and beige striped couch with a matching chair, an odd coffee table, two end tables with lamps, and a straight chair. Then Stacey's eyes focused on the picture over the couch. It was a beach scene with sunshine, foam-tipped waves, white sand, and two lovers strolling along holding hands. Smiling, Stacey looked from there to the coffee table with its arrangement of red, green, and yellow artificial flowers in a green vase. She strongly suspected that the calm and beauty were a reflection of Maila's personality.

She walked across the faded rag rug toward the kitchen table. Behind it was a window, raised several inches, allowing a breeze to slightly blow the edge of the thin green curtain. Stacey lifted the shade, gazed at the other stucco apartments, then at the garbage-laden alley below before lowering the shade to its original position.

She knew Eric had seen her gesture. She did not want to give the impression that she was displeased with her surroundings, or to behave like a spoiled American.

"Coffee smells good," she said, savoring the odor and listening to the rhythmic perking.

"It will only be a minute," Eric assured. "Cream? Sugar?"

"Cream, please," she replied, pulling out a chair to sit down. She watched as Eric moved around the kitchen, enveloped in a cozy glow from the soft light above the stove. He opened a yellow cabinet, withdrew brown mugs and a small pitcher, then returned the coffee tin to a shelf in the corner. He opened a drawer for spoons, without having to search, then took milk from the refrigerator and filled the pitcher, apparently at home in Maila's compact kitchen.

After bringing the items to the table, Eric switched off the light and sat across from Stacey. She was immediately aware of the contrast of the light behind her that reflected in his blue eyes and the dimness of the room behind him. When his eyes met hers she shifted her gaze around the room, but fearful he might think they lingered on a section where the paint was peeling, she quickly looked down, picked up a spoon and stirred her coffee.

So many questions crowded her mind about Commander Eric Farrington she hardly knew how to begin. She thought of his mention of John Carlson. "Do you also work with the Children's Fund Center?"

He sipped his coffee, then set the cup down. "Not officially," he replied. "But I help out occasionally."

He seemed almost reluctant to admit that and Stacey wondered if he "helped out" by meeting CF supporters at the airport. Was that the other reason, besides being Maila's friend that he had met her? And how friendly were he and Maila? The annoying thought persisted.

Eric was again glancing at his watch. He seemed distracted, and she realized once more that she must be an inconvenience to him. But he was stirring more cream into his coffee as if he planned to at least finish his cup.

"I believe John said you report to the Center a week from Monday. Is that right?"

"Yes," she replied, watching him sip his coffee, while hers sat steaming in the cup, much too hot to drink. "I have over a week for vacationing, sightseeing, or whatever Maila had in mind for me."

"Then you have no particular plans, or contacts other than Maila, here in the Philippines?"

A thoughtful expression crossed Stacey's face, then she shook her head. "Mom and Dad have known students from the Philippines, but Maila is my only one. She told me she'd try to take her vacation next week so we can spend the week together."

"Wonderful!" Eric exclaimed and moved his chair back slightly. "Then Maila can tell you about our plans for you, so don't unpack. But for now, I'm going to have to run." He drained his cup, then took it over to the sink and rinsed it out. "Sorry, but I have to be on duty by ten-hundred hours."

"You mean ten o'clock, I assume?"

"Right." He laughed. "Military jargon. Maila gets off work at two, and it should take her about ten minutes to walk from the hospital. So, stay put, lock the door behind me, and use this time to relax."

"I'm much too excited to relax," Stacey responded brightly.

Eric looked concerned. "Remember it's best if you stay in the apartment. Don't venture out alone. You'll have plenty of time to see the sights. Maila and I will see to that."

He picked up his hat from the kitchen countertop, placed it on his head with a slight twist of his wrist, then strode across the room. "See you," he said at the doorway, gave a mock salute and was gone.

Stacey stared absently into her coffee cup, watching the steam rise from the dark liquid. Hardly a thought had formed before the door opened, and Eric peered in again.

"You didn't lock it," he accused, as Stacey's head snapped up. "Now what would you do if someone had rushed in and begun yelling in Tagalog?"

Stacey rose from the chair, unconsciously pushing a stray lock of hair behind an ear. Laughing, she walked toward the door. "Yell back in French or Spanish?"

He shook his head. "That would never do. Especially if you smiled like that. It will be much safer if you just lock the door."

"Yes, sir," Stacey replied in mock contrition, but she secretly savored his compliment.

His voice grew apologetic. "Had I known of the emergency, I would have arranged to take the day off, Stacey."

She was touched by his thoughtfulness. "You couldn't have known," she smiled, "but I appreciate the thought. Don't worry about me. I'll be fine. You were right. I do need to rest after the long flight."

"I'm glad you're here, Stacey," he said softly.

"So am I. And I feel honored to have been assisted by an American Naval Commander upon my arrival in the Philippines. It's a very nice welcome, Eric."

"My pleasure," he assured, and stepped back. Stacey closed the door, blocking out his gaze. It was a moment longer before she heard his reteating footsteps after the lock clicked in place.

23

Stacey took off her jacket and draped it over the straight chair in the living room, then glanced toward the bags she wasn't supposed to unpack, having no idea where she would be going later. It suddenly occurred to her, that she had no idea where she was *now*.

That was not disturbing, however, and she tried to ignore the excitement brewing deep inside as she mulled over Eric's words when he said Maila—and he—had plans for her.

CHAPTER 2

STACEY WALKED TO THE DOORWAY on her left and saw that a double bed dominated the room. Going to a second door, she opened it. At least Maila had her own bathroom, however outdated the fixtures.

After getting her coffee from the table, she returned to the bedroom. The shade at the small window was partially raised. Curtains, blue-flowered on a cream-colored background, were pushed aside. Looking out the window, Stacey was confronted with an adjacent stucco apartment building. She moved to the edge of the bed and sat down, absently rubbing her hand across the printed bedspread that had known many washings.

There was an odor of aging wood, and a faint smell of disinfectant. A straight-backed chair, matching the one in the living room and the two at the kitchen table, sat in one corner. A dresser of heavy dark wood was pushed against one wall topped by a lovely lamp that seemed strangely out of place. Stacey rose to admire the delicate pink shade. Then the photos caught her eye.

Stuck in the frame around the mirror were four small photos. She drank her coffee while looking at them. The top one pictured a group of several young persons. Stacey assumed one was Maila, but couldn't be sure.

A flood of emotion engulfed her as she gazed at the next one. The picture taken at the senior banquet at college that she had sent to Maila. She and Randy looked so happy then. Deliberately, she focused on the next photo. It was Maila in her nurse's uniform. A lovely, dark-eyed, smiling girl.

Stacey remembered another photo of Maila at the age of eight, the year her parents had begun their sponsorship. The child's enormous eyes had seemed to reach out in their silent appeal of need and fear. She had not been smiling then, and though she was quite young, she appeared aged by suffering.

Being here in this country, in Maila's apartment, Stacey felt a stab of guilt at having considered her plush carpet, TV, stereo, and air-conditioning as necessities of life. *I have so much, and Maila so little*, she thought, finishing her coffee and setting the cup on the dresser.

Then her eyes swept another photo. It was of a very handsome commander in a white uniform. The smile that dimpled his cheeks was unmistakably that of Eric Farrington.

Feeling a sudden wave of fatigue, Stacey sat on the bed again. Her watch hadn't been changed to the correct time, but the small alarm beside the bed indicated it would be over four hours before Maila returned to the apartment.

With a sigh, Stacey removed her skirt and blouse, placed them over the straight chair, then lay on the bed she found surprisingly comfortable. Reaching for the side of the bedspread, she drew it up for cover. The monotonous hum of an engine droned in her ears and she felt herself drifting off.

A persistent drumming finally registered in Stacey's mind. She bolted upright in bed, her eyes widening in alarm before comprehension settled in. Someone was rattling the doorknob, then knocking and calling her name.

"I'm coming," she called, throwing back the spread, then jumped up and grabbed her blouse. She had one sleeve on by the time she reached the door in her slip. "Maila, is that you?"

"Yes, it's me," came the reply in a melodic voice, with a charming accent.

"Are you alone?"

"Yes."

Stacey unlocked the door, opened it and stepped back, finally getting the other arm in a sleeve and tried to button up.

Maila entered, her face a mask of bewilderment until she realized Stacey's predicament, then they both burst into laughter.

"Oh, Stacey," she cried, her eyes misty. "It's so good to see you."

"Even like this?" Stacey ran her hand through her disheveled hair.

"Even like this," Maila assured.

"And you, Maila. I thought this day would never arrive."

Stacey stepped forward for the warm embrace of welcome.

"You're even prettier than your photographs," Stacey complimented as she stepped back.

Stacey took in the trim lines of Maila's lovely figure clad in the neat white uniform. Her black hair was pulled back and fastened at the nape of her neck with a wide barrette. Her black eyes, moist with emotion, were nonetheless dancing with joy.

Maila sniffed, brushing at the wetness spilling onto her flawless lightly-tanned cheeks. "Oh, Stacey, you're really here! But you're the beautiful one."

Now words seemed scarce. "I wanted to make such a good impression," she shrugged, "Instead, I'm afraid I slept the morning away."

"Oh, I'm glad, Stacey. I felt so terrible that you were alone here. And I'm sure you've had nothing to eat."

"Not a bite."

"I'll see what's in the kitchen," Maila offered and headed that way.

"Then I'll finish getting dressed."

When Stacey returned to the kitchen, Maila had a pan of soup bubbling on the stove.

"It's not exactly what I had planned for today," she apologized, "but the emergency couldn't be helped. At least you got to meet Eric. What did you think of him?"

Looking away from the bright anticipation in Maila's eyes, Stacey reached over to put the coffeepot on the stove. "Very nice," she said noncommittally, "but I didn't expect to find an American the moment my plane landed."

"I knew you'd like him," Maila said, pouring soup into bowls.

"He's very special to you, isn't he, Maila?"

"Oh, yes! Eric is the most wonderful man in the world! I shudder to imagine my existence without him."

Such an exclamation did not leave much room for speculation. With a slight nod, Stacey smiled, then reached for a bowl of soup and took it to the table.

During their lunch of vegetable soup, crackers, milk, and fresh fruit, they discussed the emergency that had demanded Maila's attention, then Stacey's flight to Manila.

"Mmmmm," Maila said after a final gulp of her milk. "We'd better have our coffee while I pack. They'll be here at three."

"They?" Stacey questioned. "Where are we going?"

By now Maila was standing and stacking the dishes. "Eric didn't tell you?"

Stacey shrugged and stood to help clear the table. "There wasn't time for him to tell me much of anything—only that you two have plans for me."

Maila smiled mischievously. "Eric offered to let us spend the week at his plantation. That will give us over a week together before you start your work."

"How interesting," Stacey said with a lilt in her voice. "What kind of plantation does he have. Where is it?" She gestured helplessly with her hands. "I seem to be asking too many questions."

Maila laughed. "I know. There's so much to ask you, and to tell you. But there will be time for all of it later."

"You go on and pack while I wash dishes. If we're not coming back for a week, we wouldn't want to leave them."

"You're supposed to be enjoying yourself," Maila protested.

Stacey shook her head. "Let me do it while I'm in the mood, Maila. You'll probably soon discover how very lazy I really am."

The girls laughed. "Thanks, Stacey," Maila said somberly.

As Stacey finished clearing the table, she thought about Maila's words. Was Maila also thanking her for Eric? Eric had thanked her for Maila. He credited her with having brought them together.

She could certainly understand their mutual attraction. Just from this brief encounter, she was convinced that Maila was as lovely inside as out. She was indeed one who brought beauty to her stark surroundings. And Eric. . .

Looking at the window, Stacey thought of the

garbage in the alley and remembered a waif of a child whose dark eyes had mirrored fear and distrust. Those eyes now glowed when she spoke of Eric.

She filled the sink with sudsy water. Yes, if anyone deserved a man like Eric, it was Maila. He had so much to offer. She catalogued his virtues—he was handsome, considerate, generous, strikingly attractive in his white uniform, with the most compelling sky-blue eyes.

Yes, she thought, attacking the soup bowl as if it had a layer of burnt on crust, she could well understand why Maila would shudder to consider her existence without a man like Commander Eric Farrington.

At three o'clock Maila responded to the persistent knock at the door and the call, "It's Tomas."

She invited the two men inside, hugged the taller one, and introduced him to Stacey as her brother, Tomas Corales.

"My friend here," Tomas said, "is Orlando Molino. He is Commander Farrington's assistant manager."

The men's naturally dark skin, now deeply bronzed by the sun, and the characteristically dark hair and eyes, reflected their Filipino origins. Both wore identical denim pants with blue workshirts. But that's where the resemblance ended.

Tomas was lean and several inches taller than Orlando. His clean good looks bore a striking resemblance to Maila's more delicate features. By contrast, Orlando's rugged build gave the impression of a football player.

Tomas smiled, his dark eyes filled with warmth. "I'm glad to meet you, Miss Stamford. Our entire family is indebted to you. If there is anything I can do for you, just let me know."

Stacey was touched by his speech, uttered in slow,

halting English. The momentary uncertainty in his eyes dissolved at her responding smile. "Thank you so much, Tomas. I'll remember that."

Stacey felt that Tomas' words symbolized his appreciation for her sponsorship of Maila. Eric, Maila, now Tomas had implied that Maila's opportunities, perhaps her very life, was the result of that almost routine monthly donation.

Perhaps it was her own momentary satisfaction of having done something worthwhile that caught her off guard. The smile on her lips froze as she turned with outstretched hand to encounter Orlando's black eyes, accusingly cold.

Drawing himself up, his bulky frame stiffened and his hand slid away almost as soon as it touched hers. With stilted formality and a stiff nod, he stepped to the luggage, grasped a heavy bag in each hand, then retreated through the doorway.

With an uneasy smile, Maila eluded eye contact with Stacey and spoke to Tomas about the luggage. Stacey realized that no communication or acknowledgment had passed between Maila and Orlando.

She tried to explain it away. Perhaps he was not impolite, just reserved. Perhaps he was apprehensive about Americans, or uneasy about his English. Numerous possibilities could explain his behavior. She had met four persons since arriving in Manila. Three out of four had accepted her. She mustn't imagine storms in an otherwise cloudless sky.

Blinking against the glare of the sunlight on the cracked concrete sidewalk, Stacey's eyes adjusted to the brilliance of the afternoon sun. Several fluffy white clouds floated along the horizon and one skimmed the sun, offering a brief respite from the penetrating rays absorbed by her rust-colored blouse.

"June is one of our hottest months," Maila shrugged.

Tomas helped Orlando lift the bags into the back of the cream-colored van. Bold blue lettering across the side read, "Farrington Farms." After securing the back door, Orlando held the side door for Maila to climb in.

"Would you like to sit up front?" he asked Stacey, in perfect, fluid English.

One look at his stony face made her decision. "No. I'll sit in back with Maila." She certainly didn't want him to think she expected special treatment.

Orlando drove fast and expertly won his place in traffic on the Manila streets. Unwilling to watch, Stacey settled back against the seat, enjoying the breeze from the open window.

"Too much wind?" Maila asked as Stacey plucked the touseled strands of hair from her face.

Stacey laughed as the rush of wind caught her hair, swirling it behind her over the back of the seat. "Since we have the choice of wind or heat, I'll take the wind."

"When we get to the plantation, we can put on our swim suits and head for the pool," Maila called over the roar of traffic.

"Sounds heavenly!" Stacey exclaimed with sudden elation. "Will Eric be there?"

Maila shook her head. "He gets off duty at five. It take about three hours to drive from the base to the plantation, so it could be late before he arrives."

"What a stroke of luck," Stacey said, loudly enough for the men in front to hear. "Who would have thought that upon my arrival in the Philippines I would be escorted to a plantation, complete with a pool, and be invited to vacation there for a week."

She and Maila shared good-natured laughter, and Tomas turned and smiled. But when her gaze slid toward Orlando, she encountered his black eyes boring into her own eyes, a silent signal issuing from them, though she could not read the message.

Now that they had moved out of the rush and noise of city traffic, conversation would be easier. Stacey refused to be daunted by Orlando's attitude and decided he might simply be reluctant to open up to strangers. She would use the tactic often employed with foreign students, and take the initiative. Leaning forward, she placed her hands on the back of the front seat.

"How long have you lived here, Orlando?"

"Always," came his quick reply.

She reasoned she should ask questions that required more than one word in reply if she was to find out anything about him. "Do you live on the plantation or with . . ."

"On the plantation," he replied before she could finish her sentence.

Orlando's responses weren't impolite, just abrupt, she told herself. Uncertain as to how to proceed, she was grateful when Tomas turned toward her, filling the uncomfortable silence.

"All of Commander Farrington's workers live on the plantation," he explained. "That is, the regular workers. Sometimes extra help is brought in from the barrios."

Just then the van hit a pothole, causing Stacey to grasp the seat tightly.

"Sorry," Orlando said blandly.

She wondered if his action had been deliberate.

She slid back and settled herself against the seat, out of range of the rear-view mirror. Orlando began a conversation with Tomas in a language she did not understand. Maila's attention was focused on her folded hands against the skirt of her white uniform.

Soon Stacey and Maila were discussing the landmarks they were swiftly passing. Stacey was pleasantly surprised when Manila Bay came into view and surmised they were heading in the opposite direction than she and Eric had come that morning.

Maila explained that the city of Makati, a mile from Manila, had once been a wasteland, full of swamps. Now it resembled any modern city with its tall buildings, banks, and shopping centers. They passed the famed Forbes Park where many wealthy Filipinos lived.

In sharp contrast to the affluent sections, but in close proximity, stood one-room thatched roof huts, raised on poles, with square openings for windows in walls made of palm leaves and bamboo. Stacey asked if that were typical of the poorer sections, and Maila replied softly, "There are worse."

Stacey did not press the point, feeling Maila's answer was spoken from experience.

On that somber note, once away from city traffic and noise, Stacey was content to enjoy breath-taking views of cone-shaped mountains towering over the landscape as they traveled along the narrow island of southern Luzon. Coconut groves, fields of rice, tobacco, and sugarcane carpeted the valleys. Bamboo shrubs, stately palms, and flowering plants bordered the lakes and rivers.

"I'm afraid I'm not as familiar with the history of the Philippines as I should be," Maila admitted reluctantly.

Stacey smiled, "I understand," she replied. "My foreign students expect Americans to know all about the Empire State Building, Niagara Falls, Disneyland, the Golden Gate Bridge, and the White House. The only one I've seen is the White House, and I couldn't tell you much about that."

Maila smiled gratefully, and the time sped by while they talked about Stacey's work at the university in Illinois, their college days, Maila's nurse's training, and her work at the hospital.

Stacey was pleasantly surprised when Orlando stopped at a service station after a couple of hours.

Perhaps he was sensitive to the needs of others, she surmised, or at least his own need of exercise and a refreshing soft drink before continuing his drive. Without a word to anyone, he walked to the far end of the station and gazed toward the distant mountains.

Tomas brought 7-up for the girls. "Another hour and we'll be at the plantation," he told them. Stacey asked about his family and learned that he had a wife and two small children. She would have liked to ask about Orlando, but feared the reaction if he suspected she had inquired about him.

After another hour they came to valleys carpeted with palm fronds as far as the eye could see. "Commander Farrington's land runs for miles and miles toward Legaspi," Tomas explained. The town, situated at the foot of Mt. Mayon, Stacey learned was an important outlet for produce. "And the mountain," Thomas proclaimed, "is the most perfect volcanic cone in the world."

"The plantation is not far from here," Maila said, as Orlando turned off the main thoroughfare onto a narrow, curving dirt road that wound beneath the palms. Welcoming umbrella-like fronds shaded the occupants of the van from the still-bright rays of the retreating afternoon sun.

The serpentine road gradually climbed upward before it broadened at the Summit. Straight ahead were high, black, wrought-iron gates. A low adobe wall, topped with wrought-iron fence, extended away from both sides of the gates.

Tomas jumped out, slid back the bolt, then swung the gates inward, exposing the wide brick drive. Flowering shrubs, banana plants, and taller palms bordered the inside of the wall. Tiled walkways outlined squares of flowering beds.

Orlando pulled the van to a halt in front of the single-level structure spread out across the leveled hilltop. From the little history Stacey had read about the islands, she guessed this to be a product of the early Spanish occupation. The walls were adobe, painted white and topped with reddish-brown tile. Deep arches curved over small-paned windows, with flower boxes alive with thick green vines and brilliant red and yellow flowers.

The villa seemed to be built against the hillside. Tomas reached them and clanged a large iron bell at the entrance.

Almost immediately two women emerged from the shadows portico and the younger one, dressed in a white shirt, blue skirt, and sandals welcomed them, smiling broadly. "I am Francine." She reached for the hand of the middle-aged woman, drawing her out into the sunlight.

"This is Mrs. Molino, Orlando's mother," she said.

Mrs. Molino, wrinkled of face and slight of build, bore no resemblence to her son. Her gray-streaked black hair was fastened in a bun at the back of her head. She fixed a warm smile on Maila, but was otherwise unconcerned with the group. She spoke in Tagalog to Orlando, who answered briefly, then started the van.

Stacey was about to remind him that the luggage had not been removed when Francine reached out and touched Stacey's arm. "Miss Stamford. I be your maid. Personal."

From the corner of her eye, Stacey saw the van back into the driveway, turn, and disappear around the left side of the villa.

"First time," Francine was saying, her black eyes dancing. Seeing the joy on her round face, framed by short black curls, Stacey couldn't bear to tell her it was also her "first time" to have a personal maid.

"Call me Stacey," she said.

"Call me Francine," the woman said, as if very pleased with herself. "Come."

Entering the house Stacey passed two imposing arches, opposite each other, before following Francine down the black and white tiled hallway. The walls were lined with pictures framed in black and gold.

Ahead, Maila and Mrs. Molino conversed in Tagalog.

Smiling over her shoulder, Mrs. Molino walked through an archway on the left. Maila paused, then Francine took the lead where another hallway led off the right. "Follow me," she instructed and they ascended a narrow staircase, brightly illuminated by globes in numerous niches along the walls.

At the top of the staircase was still another hallway, extending the length of a room, with an ornate table at the far end. A gold-framed mirror reflected the vase of fresh flowers.

Francine opened a door, saying, "Yours, Stacey." They stepped inside. The bedroom was quite feminine in its blue, white, and pink decor. Against the left wall was the head of a canopy bed, topped with a frilly gauzy material matching the bedspread. Tiny pink flowers with green leaves, inside stripes of blue on a white background, covered the bed. A deep blue, furry rug lay the length of the floor beside the bed. Near the doorway stood a long white dresser, the mirror framed in ornate gold carvings. A vase of fresh flowers sat on a white table beneath an arched window between the dresser and the bed. Stacey correctly assumed Francine was responsible, for when she touched a pink blossom and exclaimed, "Beautiful!" Francine proudly said, "Thank You."

Thin pink curtains hung on gold rods at the sides of the windows, two of which were on the wall opposite the bed. Several feet into the room was a chair covered in pink velvet, with a white table beside it. On it was a delicate lamp covered with a white shade.

Francine spoke to Maila in Tagalog and Maila interpreted that the closed door on the right led to the bathroom that adjoined the bedrooms.

A small foyer on the other side of the bathroom, separated the bedrooms. A pink velvet couch sat against the wall, facing sliding glass doors that were pushed aside, allowing a light breeze to enter through the screen. Behind the couch was a rectangular picture of various pastel colors that might be an abstract of flowers, or a kaleidoscope. On each side of the painting was a white-globed light.

The low white table in front of the couch obviously matched the end table in the bedroom.

The other bedroom, in rich brown and ochre tones against a cream background exuded a definite masculine appeal. The dressers and chest were of heavy dark wood. A big double bed, covered with an orange, gold, red, and brown afghan, dominated the room.

Soon, Orlando and Tomas ascended the outside steps with the luggage and set it inside the foyer.

Francine refused any help with unpacking the bags and apologized for her English, saying, "Is not good."

"It's commendable that you speak any English at all, Francine," Stacey complimented her. "I'm afraid I don't know a word of Tagalog."

"I will teach you," Francine offered brightly. She began naming things in Tagalog.

"Wait!" Stacey protested, laughing. "I can't learn that fast! Let's take a few words at a time."

"And you will help me with English?"

Stacey felt certain that would make her a friend for life. "I'd love to," she said, then remembered Maila's mention of the pool.

She walked out on the veranda, surrounded by the railing that bordered one side of the narrow steps along one wall. Waiting about twenty feet below was a wonderfully inviting pool, like an emerald gem, the late afternoon sunlight casting shadows and a golden glow across its smooth surface. The courtyard snuggled between the back of the villa and the adjacent wing housing the bedrooms. Surrounding shrubs and stately palms provided a perfect backdrop.

Four round tables, paired with chairs, dotted the patio in vivid splashes of red, black, white, and lemon-yellow. A high lime-washed wall seemed to hold back the lush jungle that stretched toward a distant body of water. To the right, Mt. Mayon rose majestically into the sky.

"Oh, it's like a mirage," Stacey breathed appreciatively, reentering the bedroom.

"Muh . . . rahg?" Francine questioned.

"M-i-r-a-g-e," Stacey spelled slowly, then pronounced, "*Mirage*. A mirage is something that is not real, but the mind sees it because it would like to believe it is real. The pool is not a mirage, of course," she explained, "but it looks almost too beautiful to be real."

Francine nodded that she understood. "You can swim in the *mirage*."

They searched the bags. "Ah, here it is," Stacey said.

Francine looked at her questioningly.

"It's a swimsuit," Stacey explained.

"Sw . . . ?"

Stacey began to suspect that the language lessons might become one-sided. She spelled the word.

Francine's eyes danced. "The *swimsweet* is very lovely."

"*Swimsuit*," Stacey corrected.

Within moments Stacey returned from the bathroom and walked to Maila's bedroom.

Popping her head around Maila's door, Stacey implored, "Stop what you're doing and let's take a swim. You did say this is our vacation, didn't you?"

Maila turned from hanging a dress in her closet. "Oh, Stacey! You're just like I've always pictured an American girl to be. So . . . stylish."

Maila soon emerged from the bathroom, her nicely proportioned figure evidenced in a modest black suit with a diagonal red and yellow stripe from shoulder to leg.

They hurried down the narrow flagstone steps. As soon as Stacey came within sight of the pool, she ran for the low diving board, then plunged into the refreshingly cool water. She was gliding toward the side when Maila splashed in behind her and they laughingly shook the water from their faces while holding onto the sides of the rectangular-shaped pool.

"It's wonderful," Stacey said, slightly breathless from the sudden activity. It feels good to work out some of the kinks.

"You swim like a fish," Maila complimented.

"I competed with a team when I was in college," Stacey admitted. "And now that I teach there, the Olympic-sized pool is available to me."

"My brothers taught me to swim in a pond near our village," Maila confessed. "Now that I'm a nurse, I marvel that we did not all become contaminated."

Stacey laughed with her and they began to swim to the deep end. Stacey knew her own strokes were more professional, but Maila's superior strength was evident.

Next they tried the high dive. Stacey jackknifed, then slid effortlessly into the water. Maila held her nose and jumped in. Deciding that was more fun, Stacey followed suit, holding her nose, she wiggled and screamed in the air. They played exuberantly until both were exhausted, and dragged themselves from the pool when Francine came to say dinner was ready.

Still in swimsuits, they ate on the screened-in porch

overlooking the courtyard. Mrs. Molino had prepared a delicious meal of *pancit*. "Noodles," Maila explained, "with chopped shrimp, pork and vegetables." They ate mangos for dessert.

After showers and shampoos, Maila was unable to stifle her yawns, apologizing that her day had begun early at the hospital.

Stacey insisted they postpone their conversations until the next day. The tired girl slipped under the luxurious covers and her eyes drooped as soon as her head hit the pillow. Stacey returned to her own room.

After blow-drying her hair, Stacey considered seeking out an inevitable library, and returning to relax in the cozy foyer with a good book. Then a quick masculine laugh that settled into a chuckle and a few inaudible words fell upon her ears. She walked to the screen door of the darkened foyer and looked out to see that globes on high poles illuminated the pool and courtyard.

Eric, in black bathing trunks, stood talking with Francine. He turned, then his long muscular legs strode across the concrete poolside until reaching the ladder of the high dive. He climbed, with feline grace, stepped to the edge, poised, jumped high, doubled into a jackknife, then somersaulted twice before sliding into the pool. Surfacing a moment later, his muscular body and strong arms parted the water with the adeptness of a practiced swimmer.

Stacey pulled her robe close, stepped out onto the veranda, waited until he was again poised at the edge of the board, then began to applaud. "Bravo! Bravo!"

He jackknifed only, and his entry into the water was far from expert. He came to the surface shaking the water from his face and floundered around, looking in the direction of her voice. She couldn't have looked like more than a shadow from that distance and away from the focus of the light. He waved an arm high above his head.

"Come on down!" he called.

Instantly Stacey knew that was exactly what she wanted to do. However she hesitated. "I think Maila's asleep."

"But *you're not!*" he countered, and motioned again for her to join him.

CHAPTER 3

JOINING ERIC WAS THE LEAST she could do for her host, she told herself with an impish grin. Having no idea where Francine put her other bathing suits, she went into the bathroom and slipped into the wet suit she had washed and hung over the shower curtain rod. The cool dampness of the suit brought a slight shiver to her warm body. She opened the door to Maila's room. The girl's closed eyes and easy breathing indicated she was fast asleep. Stacey tiptoed back to her room and fastened on her terry robe.

Francine was wiping the colorful tables when she stepped out. "Good night for a swim in the *mirage*," she said, reaching for Stacey's discarded robe. She leaned nearer and whispered, "I told the commander about your *sweemsweet*."

After a brief moment, Stacey burst into laughter, and Francine, feeling she had said something clever, joined her.

Stacey headed for the diving board, copied Eric's initial jackknife and somersaults, then her graceful body slid into the pool with ease. With she came up for air, Eric was nearby. "That was far better than my last attempt."

"Well, you did have a little interference from the sidelines," she joked, laughing and blinking the water from her long lashes.

Finally, synchronizing their strokes, they swam to the deep end of the pool. Eric reached for the side and Stacey turned her back and hoisted herself up into a sitting position along the edge, her feet and legs dangling into the water.

She watched Eric's eyes skim the golden drops of water shimmering like beads on her skin, until they reached her own. "Again?" he asked.

"You go, I'll watch," she said.

He pushed himself away from the side, his long strokes separating the water, causing the reflection of the round globes of light to splinter across the surface of the pool, with the propulsion of his swift kicks.

When he turned and began swimming toward her again, her eyes lingered on the handsome man. When he stopped he was close enough, that with a movement of her foot, her toes could touch the curly black hair on his chest.

Resisting the temptation, she said suddenly, "Race you to the diving board."

Stacey jumped up, ran ahead, and glancing back, chided, "Last one to the other side of the pool is a rotten egg." With that she climbed the ladder, jumped from the board, wiggled her legs in the air, held her nose and plunged into the water, then churned the water vigorously with her arms and feet. She turned at the edge taking deep breaths. Her feet touched bottom and the water came to just above the top of her suit.

She searched for Eric but didn't see him, then he jumped up in front of her, splashing water in her face. She shrieked and turned her head.

"Oh, sorry," he said, but his dimples belied his apology. "Didn't realize I was so close."

She shrugged, and quipped haughtily. "That's typical of rotten eggs."

"Much fresher than a bad egg," he contradicted, his laughing eyes now a deep blue. "More like Humpty Dumpty."

Like lightning, it flashed through her mind that Humpty Dumpty had a great fall, then reprimanded herself for being so ridiculous as to analyze a nursery rhyme and a cliché.

"I wasn't really competing in your little race," he continued. "Francine said the commander would like the *swimsweet*. I was looking for it."

"Oh," Stacey said with a laugh, trying to ignore his disconcerting nearness. "We've decided to exchange a few words of English and Tagalog. I'm afraid the lessons haven't been very effective yet."

Eric's cheeks dimpled and his eyes glistened behind their blue depths. "The lesson may not be effective, but the *swimsweet* is. He learned forward and the movement rippled the water between them, causing it to play against her skin like gentle fingers. His voice was like silk floating on the suddenly still night. "The commander likes the girl in the swimsuit. Very much."

Stacey spoke with exaggerated formality, hoping to cover the tightness in her throat. "Well, thank you sir. I'm glad, because I'm looking forward to spending a week in this pool."

He shrugged, as if helpless. "A guy has to have something to attract the beautiful girls."

The crazy lurching of her heart warned that she was treading in dangerously deep waters. All she allowed herself to say was, "I doubt you have any trouble there." She brought her hands down, spraying a geyser of water between them, splashing his face.

His hands came up. "Oh, you want to play games, huh?" His voice held a playful threat.

"No, . . . I . . ." she began, then stopped as she looked into his face that had suddenly lost its dimples. A serious expression shadowed his eyes. "I think I've had enough," she admitted in a slightly uneasy voice. "Maila and I swam for a long time this afternoon."

He nodded and dropped his hands into the water. "Ask Francine to make us some hot chocolate, will you?" he asked as he turned, then swam away from her across the pool.

Stacey dried herself and glanced up at the bedroom windows. They were dark. She wondered if Maila were still asleep. Or had she awakened and looked out the window? If so, how had she felt?

She shivered in the warm night, shook the thoughts from her mind, slipped into her robe and tied the sash around her trim waistline. Then Francine appeared, eager to comply with Eric's request as she insisted, "With marshmallows!"

Stacey sat at the lemon-yellow table, trying not to be obvious while watching Eric climb the steps to the diving board, plunge into the water, and swim several more laps across the pool. How different it all was from what she had visualized her first week in the Philippines to be. Even in her wildest dreams, she couldn't have imagined a place like this, nor a man like Eric.

Soon Francine appeared with a tray laden with a pot of hot chocolate, two mugs and a bowl of marshmallows.

"Thanks, Francine. It smells scrumptious."

"*Crum. . .?*" Francine questioned. Stacey laughed, realizing the beginning of another language lesson.

Francine was still practicing the word, unable to get the first three letters together in one syllable when Eric joined them. He dried himself with the towel, then rubbed his hair vigorously until dark ringlets framed his face.

"Now Francine," he joked. "You learn too much and you'll be wanting to leave this job for a fancy city position."

Her round eyes and determined voice denied that. "No, no, Commander Farrington. That does not sound at all *crumpious* to me."

Stacey's and Eric's hearty laughter rang out together. Francine glowed with pleasure. Stacey knew she enjoyed the attention, if not the lessons.

Eric's gaze followed Francine until she entered the house, then he addressed Stacey thoughtfully. "You've certainly put her at ease. She hasn't been so happy since coming to work for me five years ago."

"She seemed a little shy at first. But she's eager for others to like her. I don't find that difficult."

"You apparently are a naturally caring person, Stacey," he commended her. "But I've known that since you were fourteen."

Stacey dropped a couple of marshmallows into her cup, covered them with hot chocolate and watched them bob to the top. "Don't be so quick to compliment me, Eric. People can fool you." She intended it jokingly and smiled over at him. "You know only a few things mentioned to Maila in my letters. Now, do you really think I would paint a bad picture of myself?"

"Don't tell me." He lifted his hand in jest. "I want to find out for myself." He looked at her intently after that remark.

Stacey picked up her spoon, stirred, then lifted a spoonful of marshmallows to her mouth. "Mmmmm, good." she murmured, licking the sticky whiteness from her lips.

She looked around unable to see beyond the golden circle of light surrounding them in the courtyard. "I

47

can see why you spend your weekends here, Eric. It's delightful.''

"Yes," he agreed. "I'm very fortunate. A couple of fellow officers and I were considering a place off base. We were in our mid-twenties at the time, with a sense of adventure, and saw the possibilities of this villa.''

"Then you're not the sole owner?''

"Thanks to financial assistance from my father, I am now," he replied candidly. "My friends eventually married, transferred to other parts of the world, and felt a greater need for the money than a piece of property in the Philippines that had been almost devastated by a flood.''

"So it wasn't a farm when you bought it?" Stacey asked, interested.

"Not after the flood. Coconut trees covered about a fifth of the property, and we were aware that this area is ideal for coconuts. When we employed native labor, cheaply I might add, to plant thousands upon thousands of the trees, we did it to cover the land. It takes seven years for a tree to mature and bear fruit, so having a farm was the farthest thing from my mind. Now, we are one of the major sources of coconuts for worldwide export.''

"Then Farrington Farms is your primary profession, rather than the military?''

"Financially speaking, yes," he replied. "However, the farm is not my first priority—not that I am averse to money," he smiled, "it's just that a bachelor has no great need for a fortune. Although I take pride in the success of the farm, I feel honored to be in the service of my country and believe in our nation's concern with the security of both the U.S. and the Philippines. It's an honorable profession.''

Stacey took a sip of hot chocolate to help dissolve the lump that rose in her throat, lowering her long lashes over her eyes. She *was* being sentimental

48

again. Yet it wasn't often she heard patriotism so touchingly spoken of.

"Well?" he said, gulping the chocolate and licking his lips, "how was your first day in the Philippines?"

"Perfect, Eric, thanks especially to you." Sincere gratitude was in her voice. "This far exceeds my expectations. And I've enjoyed hearing you talk about the plantation."

"Then tomorrow we'll tour the farms, if you like, and I'll tell you more." His smile warmed her far more than the chocolate.

"I'd love it," she assured, then drained her cup and set it down with finality. Standing, she said, "I'd better get to bed or I'll sleep the morrow away."

"Sleep as late as you like. I have some business to attend to in the morning. We can tour in the afternoon."

Stacey blotted her lips with the napkin and laid it on the tray. By that time, Francine hurried from the house, tut-tutting, and began to wipe the table where Stacey's cup had set.

"You keep waiting on me this way, Francine, and I'll turn into an insouciant bum. Good night!" She waved her hand, then looked over her shoulder with an impish grin at Eric's exasperated expression, while he attempted to spell *insouciant* for Francine.

The midmorning sun sent slanting rays of warmth through the arched windows and onto the bed, awakening Stacey to another beautiful day.

Stretching luxuriously, she sighed and smiled at her surroundings, pretending for a moment that she was a Spanish señorita in days gone by. Eager to meet the day, that had started hours before she awakened, Stacey threw back the coverlet and made her way to a window. She looked out on the landscape that she feared might have vanished during the night like a dream. It was all there. The same setting was now bathed in morning light, green palms reaching into a clear blue sky, the volcano looming mysteriously in the distance, and the languid pool.

Stacey searched the dresser drawers and found a purple swimsuit. She hadn't shampooed her hair a second time after her evening swim, so she scooped it quickly into a ponytail and secured it with a rubber band.

After washing her face and brushing her teeth, she found Francine and Mrs. Molino in the kitchen.

"I would have brought you your breakfast in bed," Francine said with a slight pout. "Oh, but you don't want to be a . . ." she thought for a moment, then continued with self-satisfaction, "a *saucy bum*."

Stacey laughed. "That's close. And before breakfast I'd like to loosen my joints with a dip in the pool."

"The *mirage*," Francine corrected.

"Right," Stacey agreed—to the native girl's delight.

Maila was on the porch, dressed in her nurse's uniform, and sipping tea from a cup. Stacey sat opposite her at the table. "You look rested this morning," she said to Maila.

Maila smiled. "I don't think I've ever slept so long. Straight through too, without waking once."

Stacey watched Maila's expression carefully. "I wasn't too sleepy last night, so after Eric came, I went down to the pool again and we swam for awhile."

Maila's smile lighted her eyes. "Yes, he told me he enjoyed spending time with you last night. He left a little while ago and expects to be back after lunch. Oh yes, he said to remind you that he promised to take you on a tour this afternoon."

"You're going, of course," Stacey said.

Maila shook her head. "I've been here many times.

And when I come, the workers have grown accustomed to my stopping by. I check on new babies, talk to some about birth control, or dispense medications. Tomas is proud of my doing this, and it pleases Eric, for it makes the workers happy. Some of them would never see a doctor if I did not encourage it." She looked down at her dress. "They see my uniform as a symbol of authority. That's why I wear it." She looked up suddenly. "You do understand, don't you, Stacey?"

"Of course, Maila. I think that's a very unselfish and wonderful thing for you to do." She shrugged. "We can postpone my tour. Perhaps Tomas or someone could drive us around next week."

Maila was insistent. "You'd have a much better time with Eric than making the rounds with me, Stacey. I wouldn't be able to explain things, half as well, and he's looking forward to showing you around. You and I can have all next week to ourselves, around the pool."

Speaking of the pool," Stacey said, rising, "I wanted to take a swim. If I don't hurry so Francine can cook my breakfast, she's going to be very upset with me."

"She feels like she's had a promotion," Maila smiled. "She's been chattering away about never having been anyone's personal maid before and wonders if she's doing right."

"This can't be real," Stacey said aloud several hours later. Dressed in white shorts and a red halter, she lay in an oversized hammock and gazed up at the tranquil blue sky. Palm leaves high above her head waved slightly as if warding off any discomfort that might reach her. Smiling lazily, she lifted her arms above her head, then entwined her fingers through the coarse mesh of the hammock.

Nearby on a round table sat a glass of ice and a pitcher of kalimansi that tasted much like lemonade – Francine's contribution to this bit of paradise at the far end of the courtyard.

She didn't hear the approaching footsteps muffled by rubbersoled shoes. Her eyes flew to the figure who grasped the sides of the hammock, encircling her in a cocoon of mesh, and began to swing.

"Eric, stop that!" she demanded. "What are you doing?"

"Paying you back," he said menacingly. "I won't stop until you spell and pronounce *insouciant* at least twenty-five times."

Her laughter rippled through the air. "It serves you right. Making Francine my personal maid! Do you realize I will have to drink that entire picture of kalimansi or her feelings will be hurt?"

He had stopped swinging. "You might try pouring it out behind a tree." His dimpled face hovered several feet above hers.

"I thought of that. She's probably watching, so cover for me." She tried unsuccessfully to rise from the hammock. "There's no graceful way to get out of here."

"Sure there is." Eric extended his hand. She grasped it and easily lifted herself to the side. Eric sat beside her, their bodies causing the hammock to sag nearly to the ground in the middle.

"Isn't this dangerous?" she asked, observing the way their knees bent nearly to their chests. It was such a humorous position she could not even feel uncomfortable about his weight pressing against her shoulder.

"Not so long as you're laughing, it isn't," he said, his dimples flashing.

"I mean," she said, giving him a sidelong look of warning, "this thing is going to break and we're going to look pretty silly."

"You already look pretty and silly," he countered.

"Eric! You're impossible!"

"Don't worry," he said. "This hammock is made from coir, a product of coconuts from Farrington Farms, or some very similar to them."

"Then it wouldn't dare break," she jested skeptically.

"That's right. This is my favorite easy chair. It can certainly hold another hundred pounds or so."

"You're very diplomatic with your 'or so,' Eric." She was thinking about the extra twenty pounds he didn't mention.

"Regardless, it's becoming," he said. "Ready to start the tour?" He shifted his weight as if to rise.

"Wait!" Stacey cried in alarm, placing a restraining hand on his arm. "If you get out, this thing will catapault me through the air like a slingshot!"

"Really, Stacey." He stood quickly, grasping her hands and drawing her gently forward with him. "Do you think I'd let that happen to you. You're imagining things."

Her laugh was soft. She was not imagining the ripples of pleasure that had swept through her body with the pressure of his strong arm against hers or when he had pulled her to her feet, and even now as they stood together close, her hands in his. Nor was she imagining the disappointment she felt when he released her.

"I'll change and be right back," she said quickly. "Slacks appropriate?"

He nodded. "Wear something on your shoulders, too," he cautioned. "The afternoon sun can give a nasty burn."

Ten minutes later Stacey rushed down the inside stairs to find Eric waiting at the foot of them. He had changed into khaki slacks and a light blue knit shirt.

"Almost twins," Stacey said, her straight hair

bouncing around her shoulders as she came to an abrupt halt.

"Hardly," he said with an admiring glance at her own khaki slacks topped by a dark blue short-sleeved blouse. "Perhaps just similar tastes."

They walked out front to the double-arched carport next to the living room. "This was one of the demolished rooms." They approached a jeep parked next to his Lincoln. "We felt it would serve us better as a carport than as an extra room."

A few yards from the villa wall were several small houses and a more impressive ranchstyle home. Children, under the obvious care of a teenage girl, ran and played with a carefree attitude. Eric pointed out the house that belonged to Francine and Jono, her husband.

"Jono cuts dried meat, called copra, from the shell of the coconut. He boasts that he can strip 1400 halves in an hour," he laughed. "I'll show you later."

They passed the ranchstyle. "Orlando lives there with his mother," Eric said. "Because of the nature of his duties, however, he often quarters on other parts of the farm."

Stacey hoped to learn more about the mysterious Orlando, and listened intently as Eric continued. "His father had a small farm near here. His reputation as an excellent farmer was well known. When our plants began to grow, he came to me, offering valuable advice about disease, irrigation, and soil. He made me aware of the possibilities here. I hired him as my manager and credit him with making our farms successful, but unfortunately, he died of a heart attack two years ago. Each of his sons has his own plot of land, including Orlando, yet they all continue to work for me."

Stacey asked if Orlando would become his manager and noted the hesitancy in Eric's voice when he answered. "He's certainly capable. His father taught him managerial skills, and sent him to agricultural and management school. However," he added skeptically, "something tells me it wouldn't be a good move right now. He seems to have become withdrawn over the past few years."

Stacey felt a little easier about Orlando. Maybe she was mistaken in thinking there was anything personal about his attitude toward her. "Is he that way with everyone?"

"That's the point," Eric said curiously. "He isn't. And he hasn't always been with me. He's very outgoing, likeable, has many friends, and the respect of the workers. I know I can rely on him as far as the farm is concerned. But he remains aloof and formal with me. I've asked him to call me Eric, but he continues to address me as, 'Commander Farrington.' Apparently, he doesn't care for my friendship."

"Not at all like Francine," Stacey quipped and they laughed together. She didn't pursue the subject of Orlando, realizing he was as unfathomable a mystery to Eric as to her.

"It may be that he resents my not caring as much about the farm as he," Eric continued in a subdued tone. He has told me numerous times how this could be turned into an even more lucrative business, if the owner put his full energies into it." Eric shook his head. "I'm not interested in that. The farm is getting too big for me now. I'm strongly considering selling the farm and keeping the villa with a few surrounding acres."

Out of nowhere, a sea of coconuts appeared and Eric stopped the jeep. He led her beneath a shaded structure where several men straddled stools with a sharp blade stapled to it. He found Jono and introduced them.

Jono's lively dark eyes lit up. "Very pleased to

meet you. Very pleased." His English was much better than Francine's. "Francine told me about you." Then he blushed furiously even beneath the browned skin. Stacey had a feeling he knew how she looked in a bathing suit.

Then he demonstrated his skills. Almost faster than the eye could see, Jono turned the coconut on the blade, tossed the meat in one pile, the shell in another. It wasn't hard to believe his 1400 per hour was an accurate estimate.

They returned to the jeep and traveled further into the palms. He stopped later near palm-thatched dwellings. "Some of the workers live in barrios at the edge of the fields, others in nearby villages. This one is located in about the center of the farm."

As they emerged from the jeep, a very old woman stepped from a doorway. She hurried to Eric and they embraced. They were introduced and Eric interpreted the woman's words that had been spoken in Tagalog.

Eric turned toward Stacey. "I told her we cannot come in, but she will be offended if we don't visit for awhile. I must ask about her children and her grandchildren. Her husband could not find work before coming here, for he's much too old. Now he is a managuite."

"A managuite?" Stacey repeated, now feeling like Francine.

"A tuba gatherer," he explained, putting the emphasis on the second syllable. "They make a delicious drink—a fermented drink—called a tuba."

Stacey nodded and smiled at the woman who was beaming at her.

As they left the barrio Eric pointed to a man with a bundle of bamboo tubes on his back.

"There is a tuba gatherer. The tubes are hung beneath the crowns," Eric explained. "They catch the sap that drips from slashes made at the base of the fronds. It would be useless to try and prevent their having the tuba that has been popular with them for generations."

Eric drove through groves where men perched high in trees, while others on the ground chopped away with machetes, separating nuts from leaves. "Nothing is wasted," he explained. "Leaves are used in roofing, packaging, and brooms. The natural fibers of the husks might end up as strainers and hats."

"And I prided myself in using coconut in a cake," Stacey said with disdain.

He smiled. "You must see these." He pulled the jeep to a stop. They got out and he knelt down to touch a few of the young trees. The tender plants stretched out across the entire valley, just begining to reach into the sky, to form their own tropical jungle.

Eric stood. "We can't begin to see it all in one afternoon." He looked at his watch. "Correction. Afternoon and *evening*. Do you realize it's past six o'clock?"

She looked at him. She hadn't thought about the passing time. But he was right. The sky was turning gray as dusk approached.

Eric did not stop at the warehouses, saying Stacey probably wasn't interested in the trucks and vans that transported their produce into Legaspi for worldwide export. "I told Mrs. Molino to expect us for dinner by 6:30."

But it was almost seven before they pulled up inside a gate that Stacey had not noticed before. A van was parked outside, and she assumed Tomas had returned with Maila.

After a few paces toward the back courtyard, Eric stopped in the shadow of the wing of the villa and Stacey paused at the sound of his voice. "Since it's late, perhaps we shouldn't take time to dress for dinner—if you don't mind the informality, that is."

57

She looked up, absorbed with the shadows playing across the angular planes of his face.

"I must apologize if I play poorly my role of host, but I don't really think of you as a guest, Stacey. You're . . ." He hesitated only briefly and added, "you're one of us."

His hand came up and his fingers touched her cheek as he gently pushed a lock of hair behind her ear, something she did habitually. A familiar gesture, but far from a familiar reaction. A feeling of euphoria enveloped her as she parted her lips to speak, but no sound came, for his hand moved ever so slowly down the fine strands of hair and his fingertips lingered on a wayward pulse at the side of her neck.

Then he spoke again, his voice low, his head bent toward hers, as if his words were of the utmost importance. "Thank you for the afternoon, Stacey. Enjoy your week here. Next weekend, we can make plans . . ."

"Sir! Commander Farrington!"

Stacey felt herself stiffen. Eric's hand moved to her shoulder, defensively.

There was no mistaking the accusing glare, obvious even in the near darkness, or Orlando's piercing gaze as his eyes moved over their faces and rested momentarily on Eric's hand on her shoulder.

Stacey shivered and Eric's hand dropped to his side. She took a step backward, hoping to be swallowed up in the shadow of the house.

CHAPTER 4

ORLANDO'S WORDS WERE FORMAL, polite, but his tone was deadly. "Tomas and Maila have gone into Legaspi with Suzanna, Lorenzo's wife. She is having trouble with her pregnancy."

"Is it serious?" Eric's concern was sincere. "Does Maila want me to meet her?"

"That won't be necessary. But Lorenzo wouldn't let Suzanna go without Maila." His voice dropped ominously, "His distrust of doctors is well known."

Eric nodded. He looked across the darkening silence at Orlando, who stood with feet apart, in the stance of one about to spring. "I'm sorry if you were inconvenienced waiting for me, Orlando," he said finally. "You could have left word with your mother or Francine."

"They said you were later than expected, sir. I thought perhaps something had happened, and I considered coming to look for you."

Stacey wondered if Eric would thank Orlando for his thoughtfulness. But apparently, he too, felt the growing undercurrent, as if they had been wayward children, now reprimanded by an irate parent. Eric did not thank him.

The instant of tension seemed eternal. Stacey shuddered to think what Orlando's attitude could cost him. She saw Eric square his shoulders and knew he was exercising the control he undoubtedly had to utilize in his military role.

"If there's nothing more. . ." Orlando said finally, as if deciding to yield to his employer.

"Not tonight," Eric replied. 'I would like to go over some of the accounts with you in the morning."

Orlando turned to leave as van lights illuminated the darkened section of the courtyard, raking their faces with its beam. The lights went off. Maila and Tomas approached, chattering happily, then Maila walked up to Eric, apologized for the lateness, explained that the situation had turned out happily.

Eric's light laughter held a note of amusement as he encouraged Maila to contain her excitement. "Dinner will be ruined, if we keep the cook waiting any longer, and *you* can't afford to be without her services."

Refusing to give in to her sudden attack of self-consciousness, Stacey stepped forward. "Does that mean Maila and I would have to do our own cooking during our vacation?"

"Exactly," Eric teased. "I'll meet you in no less than five minutes on the porch."

The girls headed for the outside entrance to their rooms. Maila asked how the tour went and Stacey began to recount the numerous facts she had learned about coconuts.

During the five minutes Eric had given them, Stacey checked her makeup in the mirror. After applying lip gloss, she brushed through her hair, tucking one side behind an ear. Questioning eyes gazed back from her reflection as her fingertips trailed down her cheek, following the path of Eric's touch.

Suddenly she dropped her hand to her lap, and held the fingers tightly with the other hand as if to restrain her thoughts. She mustn't make anything out of Eric's gesture. It was a tender moment—a way of saying he had enjoyed the day with her. Some people were naturally touchers. It was just a friendly overture. Then why the guilt, when Orlando had surprised them? But it wasn't guilt, she told herself quickly. There was nothing to be guilty about. And who was Orlando anyway, that she should be concerned about what he thought?

Determined to put the troublesome image aside, she rose from the chair. Yet it remained firmly entrenched in her mind. When he and Eric had stood facing each other, Orlando conveying some silent message she couldn't interpret, he had reminded her of a caged animal. He was the lion who pawed at his trainer. But the trainer had remained in control. Without delivering a blow, he had simply threatened with his whip. Eventually the lion had submissively retreated to its corner.

Suppose the lion attacked? She could not believe the whip would be protection enough. Suppose Eric turned his back.

How foolish! Her imagination was working overtime, just as it did when she thought for a minute there was anything more than a message of friendship in Eric's touch.

When she and Maila walked back across the courtyard, now lighted, she recalled how earlier the girl had completely ignored Orlando, and how he had slunk away. Perhaps that was the secret. Ignore Orlando.

There were something, however, one couldn't ignore. The irrational impulse of her heart at Eric's nearness. The memory of the sensation of his fingers against her cheek. And yet, all that had nothing to do with reality.

Reality was eating dinner in the informal setting of the screened-in porch, trying to focus on the lighted courtyard as if she had not seen it before, hearing Maila's pleasure in being able to help Suzanne.

Stacey could not ignore the blush on Maila's cheeks at Eric's compliment. "Maila has grown into a remarkable young woman."

Stacey swallowed hard her bite of food and smiled as Maila looked from one to the other. "It's because of the two of you, that my life is so blessed," she said, then modestly lowered her eyes to her plate. Was it only yesterday that Maila had said, "Eric is everything to me"?

She glanced at Eric and had to look away. His eyes seemed suspiciously bright and moist, yet she must be reading him wrong. Eric was grateful that she had been responsible for bringing Maila into his life. He had said so. And that's all there was to it, she reminded herself staunchly.

Suddenly aware that Eric would be leaving tomorrow, Stacey realized that he and Maila had not spent any time alone together. Only briefly did she wonder if their relationship was not as serious as implied, but then Eric dispelled that thought when he addressed Maila, without first lingering over coffee. "I'd like to hear about your visit in the villages and barrios," he said, "meet me in the library in a little while."

Maila smiled sweetly and agreed.

Protocol seemed to demand that he include Stacey. "Would you care to join us?"

As any thinking person would do, she graciously refused and excused herself, adding, "I have letters to write and journal entries to make." She did agree to allow Francine to bring a pot of coffee to her room later.

Strange she thought a few minutes later, while standing on the veranda outside her bedroom, overlooking the scene that had held such special enchantment for her last night. *Strange how deserted and lonely it looks now—just the way I feel inside.*

She set to writing the letters. There were so many—her parents, relatives, friends, students. And the journal entries. Even Francine respected her uncommunicative mood, for she quietly set down the tray, turned back the bedcovers, asked if she needed anything else, and slipped out of the room.

Stacey turned on the radio. She didn't want the interference of outside noises, in case anyone was enjoying the pool, as she had last night.

Much later, she lay in bed, the radio turned to a soft music station. The outside lights were not shining through her window. She didn't know if Maila had returned to her room, or if perhaps she and Eric were in the darkened courtyard below. But that was not her concern. She tried to think of happy days with Randy. But it was not thoughts of Randy that tormented her until she feel asleep.

Stacey heard Maila's alarm clock sound, but didn't budge until her name was called from the doorway. Sitting up in bed, she stretched her arms high. "Come in." She patted the edge of her bed.

"Sorry if you wanted to sleep in," Maila said, sitting on the bed in her nightgown. "I thought you might want to go to church with me."

"I didn't know if there was one nearby."

Maila nodded. "I would have discussed it with you last night, but when I came up and peeked in, you were so engrossed in your writing that I didn't want to disturb you."

Stacey looked down and picked at the bedcovers. There was no reason for a tinge of conscience just because Maila was considerate of her feelings. "Does the preacher speak English?" she asked quickly, looking up again.

Maila nodded and smiled. "Almost. It's Filipino English, but I think you can understand it."

"I'm sure I can. What do we wear?"

"Anything." Maila shrugged. "But keep it fairly simple. It's a village church attended by many of the farm workers. Tomas and his family. Francine. And Suzanna, the woman I spoke about last night. Also her husband, Lorenzo."

"Go ahead and take your shower," Stacey said, sliding further down in bed, pulling the sheet up to her chin. "Then I'll drag myself out of bed."

She was about to doze off when a knock sounded on the inside door. Francine entered with a tray.

"Oh, Francine, you're too good to me," Stacey gushed, propping herself up, savoring the aroma of fresh hot coffee.

Francine poured a cup, added cream, then handed it to her in bed. "You feel better?"

Stacey stared at the steaming liquid rather than at the perceptive eyes of Francine, knowing she referred to her melancholia of last evening.

"Oh, yes," she said, forcing her voice to sound casual. "All I needed was a good night's sleep."

"That's good," Francine said, turning to gather last night's coffee service.

When Stacey's glance met Francine's through the mirror, she felt a slight unease. Was there a note of sympathy in that glance and in Francine's voice? Well, there was certainly room for sympathy if she thought for a minute that Commander Eric Farrington. . .

Forcing her thoughts elsewhere, she set the cup on the side table, threw back the sheet and sat on the side of the bed.

Francine paused in the doorway. "There are hot spicy rolls keeping warm in the oven," she said before explaining she would not be at the villa again until

Monday morning. She spent Sundays with her family whenever possible.

Stacey didn't bother to curl her hair but let it hang straight, turned under at the ends, and pulled a few bangs across her forehead. She wore a two-piece suit. The black skirt was topped by a short-sleeved black and white striped jacket with a wide collar that dipped to a V in front, and fastened with black buttons and a slender black belt. She stepped into black high-heeled sandals, then pushed her hair behind one ear, exposing a tiny pearl earring. Only a light blush graced her cheeks and she applied a peach gloss to her lips.

Maila was full of compliments when she entered the room. But Stacey was struck by the other girl's loveliness. Her simple navy ensemble was the perfect foil for her dark eyes and thick wavy hair that fell below her shoulders.

"How are we getting to church?" Stacey asked as they devoured the buttery rolls.

"Eric told me last night we could take either the Lincoln or the jeep."

"I've never driver either," Stacey replied.

Maila laughed. "I'd be afraid of the Lincoln. But I know how to drive a jeep. Let's take that."

The church, a small white frame with a steeple and a cross, was situated in a village near Legaspi, close to the coconut groves. Stacey felt at home the minute she arrived, seeing people she knew in the congregation. The pastor's Filipino English was understandable and perhaps enhanced by the fact that she had to listen carefully. There was no room for wandering thoughts. The singing was lively and loud.

After the service, warm greetings came from many of the people she had seen the day before. Maila introduced her to Suzanna and Lorenzo. Jono shook her hand. She was surprised to see Mrs. Molino there since Maila had not mentioned her when she said

Francine attended. The old woman from the barrio came up and hugged her.

After they returned to the villa, Maila insisted on preparing lunch, without Stacey's help. "Mrs. Molino has everything ready," she said. "She explained it all to me last night. It's just a matter of a few minutes in the microwave."

Stacey was objecting, when Eric came to the kitchen doorway. "I've been bending over books all morning and need to work the stiffness out." He extended a hand. "Come and walk with me."

Stacey looked around at Maila. "Go on," she encouraged with a smile.

"There's something you need to learn," Eric said seriously when they were outside in the courtyard. "You should allow Maila to do little things for you. She is not playing a servant role. She feels you have given her much, and there's so little she can give you in return."

"I don't want anything," Stacey interrupted.

"Of course you don't. But don't you know she gets as much pleasure in doing something for you as you did in sponsoring her for so many years? You are her friend. Don't deny her the joy of giving."

"Well," Stacey replied, feeling properly reprimanded. "When you put it that way . . ."

His dimples appeared and his clear blue eyes indicated his pleasure. He opened the side gate and they walked out onto the dirt road. There was nothing but coconut groves, a high wall, the road, herself and Eric. They came upon a section of wall covered with a vine of shiny green leaves and tiny pink blossoms. She reached out and touched it.

"You have such a lovely place, Eric," she complimented. "And you've furnished it so beautifully."

"I can't take all the credit," he said, eyes twinkling when she looked up at him. "My villa has become a favorite vacation spot for many of my friends who have transferred, but keep in touch. Also, it seems my name and villa always come up as a possibility where the family can stay while the officer looks for housing. Inevitably," he continued, "a wife of the officer will, with tact and diplomacy, approach the subject of a wall that would be terrific with a certain kind of picture hanging there, or suggest that a green lamp didn't exactly suit a room that was otherwise pink, white and blue." He gestured helplessly and they laughed. "A few weeks later I will receive a gift. It's a mutual sharing, from which we all benefit."

Stacey discreetly changed the subject. "Do you always work on Sunday morning?"

"Rarely," he replied. "Orlando and I usually go over the accounts sometime on Saturday. Occasionally it extends into Sunday morning, but," he smiled down at her, "yesterday, I had better things to do with my time."

They had stopped at the end of the wall, where the road curved into the groves. Stacey felt the hot sun beating down on her head. The air suddenly seemed oppressive. Unconsciously she lifted her hand and pushed the straying locks of hair behind her ear. Realizing what she had done, she quickly looked out into the distance, toward the inactive volcano that loomed mysteriously into the blue sky.

With a mental shake of her head, she reminded herself that he was probably referring to the time he and Maila spent alone last night. They began to retrace their steps.

"I'll be leaving right after lunch," he said. "I try to get back to Manila for evening services at the church where, incidentally, John and Maureen Carlson attend."

Stacey recognized the names. John was director of the Children's Fund organization. Eric had mentioned that he and John were friends.

When they approached the gate, there was the sound of a spoon clanging against a glass. Eric laughed. "Sounds like a summons to lunch."

After Eric said a simple blessing for the food, he addressed Stacey. "Are you aware that I have a dining room?"

"I peeked in," she said, then with mock trepidation, added, "but I did not step a foot inside."

They laughed. She said seriously. "The dining room is beautiful and elegant. The big gilded mirror over the buffet is especially impressive. But I think I prefer dining here." She looked out over the courtyard and toward the distant mountains.

"I like its informality," he agreed. "But formal dinners are nice too. I'll call you this week and we'll make arrangements for such."

You, Stacey quickly reminded herself, *is a plural pronoun as well as singular.* Of course he meant he would call her and Maila, although he had looked directly at her when he spoke. And apparently, Maila had no difficulty in realizing what he meant, for her smile was lovely and sweet. A warm glow filled her eyes when she looked from Stacey to Eric, then back again.

Stacey couldn't ask for a more delightful place to spend a vacation, nor a nicer companion than Maila. Their activities immediately developed into a pattern. In the mornings they lolled around the pool, swimming, baking in the sun as long as they dared, then dozing in the shade until lunchtime. In the afternoons they took the jeep and Maila drove them to some of the interesting sites in Southern Luzon. They walked along the gray sands on the coast near Mt. Mayon, trekked through a fishing village, watched outriggers on the water, and visited an open market where many kinds of bananas hung from ceiling beams. The stands were laden with pineapples, papaws, nankas, and other exotic fruits Stacey couldn't begin to name.

One evening she watched Mrs. Molino prepare a dish that included shark meat.

"We're one up on him," she declared during dinner. "I used to worry that he might take a bite of me!" They all laughed and Mrs. Molino was delighted that Stacey found the meal quite tasty.

In the evening they would try their hand at making a Filipino delicacy, or lounge in a chair watching the sun set over the palms and mountains, or watch the moon rise to cast its silver glow over this bit of paradise. Stacey caught up on correspondence that she didn't expect to have time for once her work began in Manila.

After a final late-night swim and they were ready for bed, Francine indulged them in a special prepared snack and a pot of coffee. They settled down on the big double bed in Maila's room for their personal talks.

Stacey had known the surface facts of Maila's life, but it took on an entirely different aspect as Maila filled in the details.

Her mother had died of a lingering terminal illness when she was eight. That's when the Children's Fund Office became aware of the family's great need. Her older brother, Michael, was sixteen. He dropped out of school and took a job on a fishing boat. Three years later Tomas went to work at Molino farms.

"It's because of the sponsorship that I could go to school. I don't know what would have happened to me otherwise," she said gratefully. "You see, when I was fifteen, my father remarried. He said I was a big girl and didn't need him as much as his new wife and her three small children. He went to Mindanao to work at a sawmill."

A sad smile touched Maila's lips. Stacey, remembering their correspondence, asked, "That's when you went to live with your older brother?"

Maila nodded. "Michael was married then, with two children. There really wasn't room for me in that little house, though, so I helped out as much as I could. But I was determined to do well in school and not to disappoint you and everyone who gave me my chance."

"None of us expected perfection from you, Maila," Stacey said seriously, remembering that she hadn't been as conscientious in some of her own studies as she might have been.

"I demanded it of myself," she countered. "And my father took such pride in the sponsorship. I think he felt badly that it came from an organization, rather than from him, but he was glad for my opportunity. He was always advising me against things I'd never intended to do, afraid something might happen to make me lose the sponsorship."

Maila hesitated before adding, "His lifestyle is a matter of survival. Maybe someday I can help."

Stacey knew she couldn't begin to really appreciate the daily struggle for just the necessities of life. "Oh, Maila," she moaned remorsefully. "I wrote to you about all my happy times—the parties, the presents, everything."

"No, no," Maila hastened to make her understand. "Don't feel badly. That was a bright spot in my life. I read your letters over and over, and shared them with the Carlsons and Eric. I had friends, but my connection with you was special. I had a friend in America. Most of all I had hope. My life is now so much more than it might have been. Someday my own children can have a good life. That's part of what you and Eric and the Carlsons have given me."

Stacey reached over and placed her hand on Maila's for a moment. "I'm proud of you. Eric is. Anyone would be."

Maila's smile warmed her heart. She knew their

friendship was confirmed and could be lasting and abiding. The only factor that dimmed such a prospect was her own errant feelings for Eric. He meant everything to a woman who had so little of life's joys in the past, but deserved them all. She refused to question the personal relationship between Maila and Eric. To ask out of curiosity would be a betrayal rather than a sharing of confidences. Yet, it was Maila herself who paved the way for intimate discussion.

"Do you think you and Randy will get back together?" Maila asked.

"It's over," Stacey said with finality. It wasn't easy acknowledging that a two-year relationship had ended on a sour note.

She told Maila about Randy's coming to the college as a professor of psychology, during her senior year. It was wonderful at first and she believed marriage was in the offing. When he didn't live up to the image she had created in her mind, she refused to face it. Such attention from Dr. Randall Kemper was flattering. "While I was outgrowing my attraction for college students, Randy was becoming increasingly attracted to them," she admitted.

It hadn't been Randy's association with other women that bothered her so much, but the pain of his dishonesty. After a moment of silent struggle, she sighed. "We can never go back to what we had before. He was uppermost in my thoughts for almost two years." Her voice trailed away. "But not anymore."

"There's so much more to consider than whether or not you love someone, isn't there, Stacey? We have obligations to our families, and to other people, not just our own personal feelings."

Stacey knew she would not be personally attracted to a man who didn't possess certain qualities. But she had never thought in terms of family obligation. Maila would. Her situation was different.

"When I was seventeen, my life could easily have taken a different turn," Maila said distantly. "I became terribly infatuated."

Stacey braced herself for the discussion about Eric. "He had taken an interest in me. As soon as I was old enough and skilled enough, I helped the Carlsons in the office. They knew of my interest in nursing, but there was no money for it. After my high school graduation, Eric said he would pay the tuition for my nurse's training, including dorm fees."

Her eyes shone with moist gratitude. "It was totally unexpected. My father behaved as if I had performed a miracle, saying that if I were careful, I had Commander Farrington to insure my future. I didn't realize the implication at the time."

Stacey rose to pour another cup of coffee, then sat in a chair, shadowed in the lamplight. From over the rim of her cup, she watched silently, waiting for Maila's disclosure of some indiscretion she apparently wanted to divulge.

Maila leaned against the pillows at the head of the bed, her face partly shadowed, partly bathed in light. After a moment of reflection, she took a deep breath, then with determination, began.

"It was during the months between high school and nurse's training. Tomas and Orlando had become friends. They came into Manila on weekends or special occasions and sometimes would take me with them to the movies, or to eat, or to a festival. Sometimes it would be the three of us. Other times Tomas would have a date. I never thought anything about it. I was seventeen. Orlando was twenty-four. We had a wonderful time together. We talked easily. He said I was very smart and," she blushed, adding low, "and beautiful."

"You are, Maila," Stacey assured, feeling strange about the direction of the conversation.

"When Orlando said things like that, I accepted it as I would from a brother. One night on the way back from a comedy movie, we were laughing and joking. Gina sat next to Tomas in front. Right in the middle of a laugh, Orlando reached over and took my hand in his. My laughter stopped. All I could do was swallow, and swallow, and swallow."

Maila snickered, then they both burst into laughter. Then Stacey apologized for her outburst. "It's not really funny," she said, brushing at her tears with the back of her hand. She could imagine how frightening such an experience must have been for an innocent young girl.

"It's funny now," Maila agreed. "But not then. I had never seriously thought about myself and a man. But I began to. I started to notice how handsome Orlando was, and think about how much fun we had together. Then one night he came alone. When he turned to me, I knew he was going to kiss me. I was afraid, for I was just a girl, and he was a man. But when his lips touched mine, it was so sweet and gentle I wondered if he had ever kissed anyone before. Then he asked me to marry him."

"What did you say?" Stacey prompted, leaning forward in the chair, trying to fathom the meaning of this incredible revelation.

"I didn't say anything for a long time. He said he would talk to my father and Michael about it, and that Tomas already approved."

"You . . . wanted to marry him?" Stacey asked, trying to keep her voice evenly modulated. She realized Maila was talking about an infatuation not with Eric, but with, of all people—Orlando Molino.

"More than anything," she admitted. "That thought blocked out everything for a while. My future, my nurse's training, my obligation to other people. All I could think about was being in his arms and having him kiss me."

Stacey smiled at her. "So he talked to your father and Michael?"

"Yes, and when he came to tell me what they said, he apologized, saying he had not known that Commander Farrington was waiting for me to grow up. That had never occurred to me," Maila said now. "A lot of things never occurred to me before. But Orlando stood there, in the doorway. He wouldn't even sit down. He said he had nothing to offer me except his love, and that was not enough. If I married him, he could not allow Eric to send me to school. I would have to live with his family until he could make enough money to pay my fees, or I would have to work and attend evening classes."

Stacey's eyes grew wet, seeing the moisture that crept down Maila's cheeks.

Maila drew in a deep breath. "He told me he would not destroy my future, for he knew my ambitions, and to marry him would only make me grow to resent him. He said he would not deprive me of the opportunities and kind of life that Commander Farrington apparently wanted to give me, and promised not to interfere again."

"And he didn't?" Stacey asked, watching Maila's silent struggle.

She shook her head. "That was seven years ago. He went away for several months. No one knew where he was, except Tomas, and he wouldn't say. When Orlando returned, he was different. You see how he is. He doesn't even like me now. He will not even speak."

"You're no longer infatuated with him?"

"It's probably like you said about Randy. You can't return to earlier days. I grew up overnight in a sense and had to consider what Orlando had implied about Eric. How could I choose Orlando if Eric were waiting for me to grow up?"

Stacey rose and set her cup on the tray and deliberately wiggled her shoulders in a stretching motion. How, indeed, could anyone choose Orlando Molino over Commander Eric Farrington?

"You're tired," Maila responded predictably, noticing Stacey's stifled yawn. "We'd better go to bed."

They said goodnight and Stacey went to her own room. She knew Maila could have talked longer. But Maila wasn't seventeen now, with her touching story about how she felt when Orlando kissed her. Stacey didn't want to hear about later, when Commander Farrington insisted she call him Eric. Or when he made his intentions clear.

She stood in the criss-crossed arch made by the silver moonlight as it poured through the window. She didn't really notice. She was thinking that she already knew too much about Eric Farrington. The sound of his voice, the touch of his hand, the blue of his eyes.

CHAPTER 5

On THURSDAY EVENING. Stacey and Maila lazily lounged in the courtyard long after their dinner had settled. Respectfully, they waited for the reflection of pale pink, blue, and gold of the sunset to fade from the pool before disturbing its tranquil surface.

Suddenly, the outside lights came on. Creeping shadows disappeared. Drooping eyelids opened wide. Francine joined them on the patio and handed a written message to Stacey.

"I hope I got it right," she said with uncertainty. "I had Commander Farrington spell the words, but he said not to disturb you."

Stacey read the message to Maila. Orlando would take them to Maila's apartment on Friday afternoon. He invited them to take a cab, join him, John and Maureen Carlson at a restaurant in Manila. He gave the time and location, along with his officer's quarters phone number for them to call in case of conflicting plans.

The following afternoon around four o'clock Orlando dropped them off and made two trips up the flights of stairs with the luggage. His parting glance in Maila's direction would have gone undetected by Stacey, had it not been for their earlier conversation about him.

His angry eyes swept her way, as if daring her to comment. Her intended "thank you" went unspoken and she realized he had left her staring at the door, remembering her own anger with Randy. It wasn't that she disliked Randy. It had been because she cared so much, and had been hurt. Was it possible that Orlando was not really angry, but hurting?

"We have about three hours," Maila was saying, after peering through the bedroom doorway to look at the clock.

"I'll take that long," Stacey said disdainfully, feeling hot and sticky. She ran her fingers through strands of hair she hadn't bothered to shampoo after the morning swim. "That wind-blown drive for hours in a Farrington Farms van leaves something to be desired." They laughed. "You go first," she prompted Maila. "Your hair takes longer to dry. By the way, what sort of restaurant is it?"

"One of Manila's finest," Maila replied. "Not necessarily formal, but very nice. Eric and the Carlsons took me there after my college graduation. I'll wear my best dress," she said, emphasizing *best*, as if there were only one.

While Maila showered, Stacey unpacked a few of her clothes, taking out the dress she would wear. She had bought it last Christmas, wanting something to make her look more grown-up and impress Randy when they went to parties with his faculty friends. She hadn't realized then that his tastes were reverting to younger girls. Now, she realized she hadn't wanted to admit to all the signs that indicated she and Randy were not perfectly matched.

Sighing, she laid the dress on the bed, deciding it did not need to be touched-up with her travel iron. She hadn't brought the matching long-sleeved jacket, knowing there would be no need for such in the Philippines.

Two hours later they were ready. Stacey wore her rich brown figure-hugging silk dress that fell to just above her knees. Thin, metallic gold straps over her shoulders matched the narrow belt at her small waist. Her high-heeled sandals were the same color as the dress.

She curled her hair, including the bangs. Tawny waves, with rich golden highlights swept down one side of her face to her shoulders. The other side was tucked behind a delicate ear, exposing a rectangular earring, matching the straps of her dress.

While Maila dried her long hair, Stacey sat at the dresser where she set up her make-up mirror. She applied a light sprinkling of gold eyeshadow over the richer brown that gave depth and sparkle to her eyes. A bronze blush and lip gloss finalized the effect. Stacey stood and turned, appraising herself in the mirror. *Better than Christmas,* she told herself, pleased with the tan she had acquired, and realized her eyes were dancing. *Excitement,* she explained to her reflection, *over the prospect of meeting the Carlsons. That's all it is.* Then she added, *It has to be.*

Maila switched off the dryer. "You sparkle," she said with genuine admiration.

"Thanks to this," Stacey retorted, gesturing toward her make-up kit, realizing she could never graciously accept a compliment.

"I'll have to get one," Maila said, smiling.

"Use mine," Stacey offered.

Maila shrugged uncertainly. "I never use much make-up. There aren't many such occasions."

"Let's see what you're wearing."

Maila put on a royal blue satin dress cut straight across from shoulder to shoulder. The elbow-length sleeves were typical Filipino butterfly wings made of Spanish lace.

"Fabulous," Stacey said sincerely. "Now sit down."

Maila expectantly obeyed her playful command.

First, Stacey brushed her wavy hair away from her ears and applied spray. She had Maila put on a pair of her own crystal earrings that would pick up the blue color of her dress.

She applied a touch of blue eyeshadow. "This will make your eyes soft, yet mysterious."

Maila smiled, as if Stacey were exaggerating.

A small amount of contour, then blush, gave an oval shape to Maila's more rounded features. "Put on your lips," Stacey said, handing her a tube of raspberry gloss.

Maila stared at the completed picture. "Thank you," she breathed, still studying herself in the mirror, as if just beginning to realize how truly lovely she could be. Stacey remembered her saying that Orlando told her the same thing when she was seventeen. Eric undoubtedly had, too. If not, tonight would present the perfect opportunity.

"If we don't hurry, we'll be late," Maila gasped, rising from the chair.

"We're worth waiting for," Stacey joked.

Maila giggled. "You may be right," she agreed, with a confidence that Stacey hadn't detected before. Then she called a cab.

When they entered the foyer of the restaurant, Eric was there. His admiring glance swept over them. "What did I do to deserve two such beautiful women?" he complimented.

"Who says you deserve them?" said a bantering female voice. A woman in a cream-colored dress, wearing a single strand of pearls, stepped over to them. "You've got to be Stacey," she said before Eric could reply with whatever retort must have been on the tip of his tongue, or could even make introductions. Stacey was amazed at the woman's short, curled, cinnamon-colored hair.

"I'm Maureen Carlson," she said, her dark brown eyes scanning Stacey approvingly before hugging her. Then she stepped back, reaching for the sleeve of a man's charcoal gray suit.

"My better half," she said. "John Carlson."

While Maureen hugged Maila and commented on her appearance, John and Stacey shook hands. Stacey was acutely aware of the number of years she had admired John Carlson. She'd thought of him as the intermediary between her and Maila, and had respected him tremendously for devoting his life to such a work and being a blessing to so many people.

He looked to be about forty, as tall as Eric, but not as muscular. Graying hair and a serious expression gave him an air of distinction.

But when he said, "I've looked forward to meeting you, Stacey," his deep voice and warm smile convinced her his statement was not for the sake of courtesy.

"And I'm grateful for the opportunity to work with you this summer, Mr. . ." Frowning, he shook his head. "John," she said.

He nodded approvingly.

Feeling a hand at her waist, she turned to see Maureen beside her. "We've known and loved you for a very long time, Stacey," she said warmly. "Welcome."

Stacey felt a lump in her throat and could hardly get her "thank you" past it. How could she ever live up to the ready confidence and friendship these people offered her?

"Perhaps we should continue our conversation at the table," John suggested, smiling. Eric looked up from an intense discussion with Maila and led the way to the entrance of the dining room. Then he stood aside as each of them passed to follow the maitre d' through a maze of round tables.

Crystal chandeliers cast varying shades of golden shadows around the spacious rooms, redolent with the mingled aromas of spice, herbs, strong coffee, and expensive perfume.

In a far corner, a pianist played classical music, accompanied by the faint clink of silver, soft laughter, and swift, sure footsteps of waiters bearing huge silver trays laden with food.

Aware of Eric behind her, Stacey suddenly realized she hadn't really looked at him. With her eyes closed she could accurately describe the entire party from head to toe, including the maitre d' in his black pants and red coat with gold braid—everyone, that is, with the exception of Eric. She recalled only blue eyes and dimples when he smiled.

Eric seated her beside John, then took his place between her and Maila.

Now while he was concentrating on the maitre d', Stacey allowed herself the luxury of studying him in profile. He was wearing dark blue trousers, a white dinner jacket, light blue silk shirt and a navy bowtie. She'd always thought of bowties in connection with small boys or wedding parties, but realized that nothing so trivial as a bowtie could detract from Eric's masculine appeal.

Her eyes traveled to the firm lean thrust of his jaw. From there it was only a flicker of an eyelash to his waiting gaze. Her pulse quickened to find him watching her. "That's a lovely tan." he smiled at her heightened color. "I trust you enjoyed your vacation at the villa." The blue sky was in his gaze as it moved slowly over her shoulders and face, warming her skin like the sun.

"It was perfect, Eric," she said sincerely. "So was Francine. We said a very tearful goodbye."

"Then you'll have to return to the villa soon."

"Say when," she retorted as if the notion were not a near impossibility.

To her surprise, Eric already had plans underway. "Two weeks from tomorrow," he invited. "It's a party, and something we need to work out with John and Maureen."

"Isn't it lovely there?" Maureen's question was more a statement of fact.

Then they were all talking about the villa. "It wasn't until yesterday when I was reading a history of the Philippines that I discovered Mt. Mayen is not inactive," Stacey said with chagrin.

"The last time it erupted was in '45, I believe," John added.

"But it always gives warning," Eric said defensively, as if its dubious status were a criticism of his villa. "Where there's fire, there's smoke."

"Shouldn't that cliché be reversed?" Maureen asked.

He spread his hands and shrugged his shoulders. "Same thing." Then he looked at Stacey and she detected the mischief in his eyes. "Did you also read about our typhoons?"

"Yes, I did They sound like our own tornadoes in Southern Illinois. We lose our roofs, our trees."

"They've certainly done damage here," John interjected seriously.

Maila attempted to dispel the sudden pall. "On this island they usually hit north of Manila."

"How did we get sidetracked?" Maureen teased. "We'll never be able to digest our food, worrying about erupting volcanoes and devastating typhoons."

"Blame Stacey," Eric tossed out. "It's her history lesson."

"On the brighter side," Stacey countered, "I also read that 80 to 90 percent of the people in the Philippines are Christians." She looked at Eric triumphantly. "Can you argue with that?"

"Of course he can't," John said, taking her side in the light-hearted bantering. "That's due to the influence of the Spanish during their occupation; then, later, the Americans."

"Fortunately, so is the food," Eric added as the waiter set menus before them.

"I have nothing against Filipino food," Stacey assured, leaning forward slightly. "Mrs. Molino went out of her way to prepare delicacies I'd never tasted. Like water buffalo, shark, and fried bananas. It was . . . well . . ." she glanced toward Eric, then back at the others, ". . . different."

They laughed with her. "But tonight," she said firmly, leaning back and opening the menu, "I have a strong urge for something totally American."

"My sentiments *exactly*," Eric echoed meaningfully, and she looked at him sharply. He grinned at his menu.

"Oh, I almost forgot," Maureen gasped, a note of chagrin in her voice, "This came for you today." She held out an envelope.

Eric reached for it and passed it to Stacey. She stared at it for a moment. He must have written it even before she left the States for it to have arrived so soon. Why did he write? There was nothing more for him to say.

"I'm sure everyone will understand if you want to go ahead and read it, Stacey," Eric said seriously.

It took no effort at all for him to glance down and see, in bold black letters, the return address in the upper left-hand corner, Dr. Randall Kemper.

Stacey shook her head and folded the letter. "It can wait," she said quietly, then slipped the letter into her small gold bag.

Eric leaned toward her with his menu. "The T-bone is excellent." His finger moved to the sirloin tip. "Or this," he said, his head turning and she looked up. Their eyes locked for a moment. It was as if he had said, *If you need someone to talk to, I have broad shoulders.*

Reaching up, she needlessly made her hair-behind-ear gesture. His smile was warm, then he turned to Maila and asked if she had decided on her order.

The T-bone excelled Eric's predictions, as did the baked potato Stacey generously filled with both butter and sour cream. She was delighted, too, with his suggestion of a side dish of hot salad, consisting of tender pea pods, scallions, and carrots cooked in hot oil and garlic. Everyone seemed to be as hungry as she, attacking each dish with great concentration.

When the conversation resumed, they wanted to hear all about America, Stacey's work at the college, her life in Carbondale, the latest music, TV shows, fads, and life in general.

"We get back to the States a couple of times a year," John explained. "Once to visit family, and again for the annual organizational meeting. As much as we love it here, we still miss our native country."

Stacey could understand that. Only a week had passed since her arrival in the Philippines, but she was becoming increasingly aware of all she had taken for granted in America. The conversation steered clear of serious matters, and Maureen mentioned they really should get out more often like this. Stacey considered how busy their lives must be. Eric had a business to oversee, in addition to an important position at the base. Maila's nursing knew no strict hours, requiring her to work on weekends, and to be available during emergencies. John and Maureen were so closely involved with the personal lives of people, they would ultimately be on call at all times. Stacey began to feel that her summer's work might be more demanding than she realized.

Stacey refused any of the exotic-sounding desserts and asked if they had any chocolate ice cream with hot fudge syrup. The restaurant could indeed oblige her, the waiter informed. It sounded so good everyone at the table decided on the same, except John and Eric asked for vanilla.

"With a cherry on top," Stacey emphasized and the waiter nodded.

Since Maila had to be at work on Saturday at 6 a.m., it was decided that Stacey would spend the night with the Carlsons and move into her apartment the following day.

"I'll drive her and Maila to the apartment," Eric offered.

"You first," Stacey said after Eric unlocked the front door of the Lincoln. Maila climbed in.

A few minutes later they arrived at the apartment. Her luggage was again lugged down three flights of stairs and loaded into the trunk of John's car.

Stacey and Maila embraced. Then she turned to Eric. "Thank you for the vacation, the dinner. . . for *everything*."

"My pleasure," he assured and held the car door while she climbed into the back seat. He closed it and leaned down to the window.

"Don't forget your letter," he said, glancing at the gold bag on her lap.

A moment of incomprehension touched her face. "I had already forgotten," she admitted. A tiny laugh escaped her throat as her lips spread into a smile. She expected to see his cheeks dimple and his eyes twinkle with encouragement.

But his face was serious and his eyes shadowed so they were almost black as they scanned her face and down to where the pale moonlight filtered into rest on the gold strap across her shoulder.

"I'll be in touch," he said softly, then moved away. She, John, and Maureen lifted their hands in farewell as the car pulled away from the curb.

Glancing back at Maila and Eric, standing on the sidewalk, waving at them, she thought about what wonderful people they both were. And what an attractive couple they made. John turned the corner. Stacey staightened in the seat and looked down at the bag she clutched in her fingers.

She knew what Randy would have to say. Another apology, no doubt. The other woman had meant nothing. Temporary distraction. How sad, she thought, for the other woman, whose affections Randy had taken so lightly.

On Sunday morning, wearing the same outfit she wore to church near the villa, with the addition of a white milanette straw derby with a black taffeta band and bow, Stacey climbed into the back seat of John's car.

"You look as if you had no trouble sleeping in a strange bed," Maureen commented, glancing around at Stacey. Her red hair was partially covered with a small navy blue hat with a tiny veil at the forehead, matching the navy blouse she wore with a white suit.

"Slept like a log," Stacey responded truthfully. "It's great moving into a furnished apartment." That had been done yesterday. It wasn't as luxurious as her American apartment, but far exceeded the bare essentials of Maila's. It was perfectly adequate with its small sitting-dining area, bedroom, bath, and compact kitchen. They had bought groceries and incidentals. Maureen said the apartment had been cleaned a couple of days before. After unpacking she settled down to a sandwich supper and watched a program on the small TV she didn't expect would claim much of her attention during the summer.

Although refusing Maureen's invitation to supper on Saturday night, she promised to eat lunch with them after church.

"We have to make a little side trip," John said, driving out of Manila and heading north.

"Fredrico meets us beside the main road," Maureen added. "He's nine years old and . . . oh, there he is now."

Stacey looked out to see a little boy in a tan shirt and long brown pants walking beside the road, strumming on a ukelele and singing at the top of his lungs. When he saw them, he stopped, waved the ukelele high in the air and a happy smile spread across his face.

He jumped into the back seat, slammed the door and perched on the edge, turning to regard Stacey from head to foot. Maureen introduced them.

Fredrico shoved his hand forward. "Mr. and Mrs. Carlson told me about you, but not that you were so pretty." He pumped her hand.

"Well, thank you," she said, glancing at Maureen who grinned. "And I'm glad to meet you, too, Fredrico." She could have said she had never seen a more handsome young boy, with such huge black eyes, or with such a winning smile.

"And I'm glad you're here," he replied with a sincerity that surprised her. "My people sure need good Christians like you."

After another flash of brilliant white teeth, he let go of her hand, settled back against the seat and crossed a foot over one knee.

Maureen looked back. "Where are your socks, Fredrico?" she asked intimidatingly.

His foot immediately hit the floor and he tried unsuccessfully to tug his pants over his ankles.

"You gave them away again," she accused. "Didn't you?"

He exhaled audibly and nodded, looking at his scuffed dusty shoes.

"How many times must I tell you, Fredrico?" Maureen implored. "You mustn't bribe other people into going to church." She caught John and Stacey exchanging amused smiles.

With head still bent, Fredrico turned his face toward Stacey, gave her a sidelong look of determination, then nodded his head as if to say, "Yes, he must."

He grinned, then reached over for his ukelele and began to strum a tune. "Know this?"

"The first song I ever learned," Stacey replied.

During the remainder of the short drive, the two of them sang "Jesus Loves Me," and she taught him another verse that he hadn't heard.

"May I sit with you after Sunday School?" he asked, looking up at her after they emerged from the car in the parking lot.

"I'd like that," she agreed. He bounded away. Stacey turned to John and Maureen, who smiled.

Fredrico sat so still during the worship service that Stacey looked over to see if he had fallen asleep. He was watching the pastor with intense concentration.

It was a beautiful brick church, much like the churches in any American city. Of modern design the sanctuary was carpeted and had stained-glass windows and a raised choir loft. The middle-aged pastor, a tall Filipino who wore glasses and appeared quite dignified in his dark suit and conservative tie, spoke eloquently in impeccable American English.

In her Sunday School class Stacey was pleasantly surprised to find several American women whose husbands were stationed at the naval base. Then after the service she felt almost overwhelmed by many eager to know about the work she would be doing in the Philippines.

"So you'll be working with Mr. and Mrs. Carlson all summer?" Fredrico asked, after they left the church.

'For about eight weeks," she said smiling.

"Will you get paid for it?" he asked solemnly, his black eyes searching hers.

What a strange question for a little boy to ask. It crossed her mind to say that in a way she was paying to be here. The tuition for the college credit she would receive toward her master's degree. The plane fare. She would get the apartment rent-free in exchange for her services, but no salary.

"No, I won't get paid for it, Fredrico," she answered after only a moment's hesitation. "But you need to understand that some people must get paid for their work, or they wouldn't be able to take care of themselves, or to help other people."

'I know that," he said immediately. "Mr. Carlson explained it to me. But I know it anyway. You see, I'm going to be a preacher, and I expect to get paid because I will have to feed my family if I have one. And I want to help other people." His determined eyes bore into hers. "But I won't do it for the money," he assured, shaking his head from side to side.

"Why is it important to know, Fredrico? Don't you think I could care about people as much if I got paid to do the work?"

He nodded and looked down at the toes of his worn shoes. "Yes, m'am. I wanted to know so I could tell my daddy."

He said no more and Stacey thought it was because his throat wouldn't allow it, for he swallowed hard,

89

then lifted his head and gazed out the opposite window, as if he were trying to rid himself of the moisture that had quickly formed in his black eyes.

Later, after helping with the preparations, she sat down to lunch with John and Maureen. "The spirituality and friendliness of the people at church is marvelous," she said after grace, and helping herself to fried chicken. "I've heard that churches have personalities. This one definitely does."

Maureen nodded in agreement. "The people and pastor have been a great blessing to us. We need the kind of spiritual intake we receive there to enable us to meet the personal demands of our job."

"That sounds like my need for breaks and summer vacation," Stacey said with a smile. "As much as I love my counseling and the studies, I need to get away from them in order to go back refreshed and enthusiastic."

"That's something you'll have to watch out for here, Stacey," John warned. "Remember to take time for yourself and your needs. It's all too easy to become wrapped up in the personal lives of these people and their problems."

"I can imagine," Stacey replied. "Already, I think Fredrico has stolen my heart. He looked at me with those huge black eyes, so inquisitive, yet so determined. He spoke to me like a little man, saying how much I was needed here." She shook her head, amazement in her voice. "You'd think a little boy would be running around getting into mischief, playing ball, or something."

"He's certainly capable of all that," John said with a laugh and Maureen nodded in agreement. "But you're right, Stacey. That little boy . . ." His words trailed off and his gray eyes studied her thoughtfully. "Tell you what," he said finally. "I think we'll assign Fredrico's case to you."

Stacey's momentary jubilance diminished when both John and Maureen looked at each other, then at her. They smiled but she sensed some distant concern.

Stacey lingered after dinner enjoying the Carlson's home in a nice residential area so much like her parents' in Carbondale. Later Maureen drove her to the apartment, saying she would pick her up for church that evening.

The apartment was only a couple of blocks from the Children's Fund Office, so she wouldn't need transportation to work. But she missed her car. Maila should have gotten off work at two, so she called her. They chattered for awhile about the two days since they had seen each other and decided to get together on Maila's next day off. Stacey asked if she were going to church and she said yes, she attended a small church within walking distance of her apartment.

After hanging up, Stacey searched her closet, wanting to change from what she had worn that morning. Deciding on something soft and feminine, she chose a pale pink knit dress with a straight skirt and blouson top with short full sleeves and bateau neckline.

She unfastened her hair from the topknot she had worn under the derby and brushed it around her shoulders, tucked one side behind her ear, then put on a gold choker and matching earrings.

While applying pink lip gloss, she admitted it. It had been running around her mind all afternoon. *I wonder,* she thought, *if Eric will be there tonight?*

He was. They saw him in the parking lot and waited. Somehow the two of them lagged behind John and Maureen. He said those ridiculous, joking things she couldn't take seriously.

"Francine sends her regards," he said. "We both missed you."

91

'You're the one who summoned me back to Manila,'' she said saucily, looking up at him.

''You're right,'' he agreed, his cheeks dimpling. ''But you were at the villa in spirit, if not in person. I kept seeing Stacey splashing me in the pool, struggling in the hammock, pouring out Francine's kalimansi behind a tree.''

He steered her, laughing, into the church. She could have added to his list, but not aloud. He sat beside her and they shared a songbook. It wasn't until after the pastor began his sermon that Stacey thought of how many preachers she had heard joke about their congregation's wandering minds. Could they really be so naïve or unimaginative to believe those minds worried about a roast burning in the oven?

CHAPTER 6

ON MONDAY. Stacey remained in the field office, becoming acquainted with personnel and procedure, files and paper work that had to be expedited. When Maureen put on her reading glasses, Stacey felt she had rolled up her sleeves and said, "Let's get to work."

Wanting to familiarize her with all phases of the operation, Maureen had her help with opening and sorting of the enormous stacks of mail, explaining along the way.

Checks had to be readied for deposit, recorded, and applied to different funds like education, specific needs, birthday gifts, while other contributions were left to the discretion of the office. A monthly accounting had to be prepared to send to each sponsor.

Hundreds of questions required answers, not only about sponsored children, but about the organization itself. Letters from sponsors came from all over the world, many to be translated into English or Tagalog.

"These will be taken to the child for a response,"

Maureen told her. "That's where you will be of particular help." Stacey smiled. That appealed to her.

A few sponsorships had to be cancelled. "What happens to the child then?" Stacey asked.

"Sometimes we're able to apply a new sponsorship to a cancelled one. And, when that is impossible, or someone cannot send a pledged amount for a month or so, we have several private citizens who take up the slack." Maureen looked up from the desk. With a smile, she added, "Like Eric."

Stacey's mind tumbled backward to the time she was fourteen and had sent partial payments for a couple of years. "Then," she questioned thoughtfully, "someone had to supplement when I didn't pay the whole amount?"

"That's right," Maureen replied. "The families are dependent upon a promised amount each month. It can mean the difference between being well fed or going hungry."

"Such poverty is alien to me," Stacey said distantly, hardly able to grasp it even now.

"I'm sure you've heard people say that the poorest in America are wealthy by the poverty standards in some countries." Maureen continued. "It's quite true. Fortunately, people's hearts are touched by our pleas for help on TV and through pictures of needy children, and they respond generously. But it does have a greater impact when you see poverty first-hand, watch a young child's bloated belly because of malnutrition."

"And when I think of all the things I've wasted," Stacey began in self-recrimination.

"Now, Stacey," Maureen began, pulling off her glasses. "I feel sure the Lord wants us to enjoy this world's goods. Yet, He expects us to share. If you had divided everything equally with Maila, you would both be struggling in poverty. The way it happened, you gave out of your abundance and enabled Maila to become a self-sufficient, self-supporting young woman. If everything were handed to her, she couldn't take pride in having used your gifts to advantage. It is the fact that you provided the opportunity, and she took advantage of it, that makes such a wonderful success story."

Maureen put her glasses on again and turned to the mail. "That's what we do here, Stacey. We help others help themselves."

"Of course you're right," Stacey relented. "For a while I reverted to childhood, feeling guilty over eating a hamburger because children in India were starving."

Maureen laughed and quickly explained. "I, too, have been a victim of such attacks of guilt. Let's take a break."

Over coffee in her private office, Maureen shared some of her own life. "I had such a martyr complex when I went to work at the office in the States. It was John who pointed that out to me. He told me that God doesn't want us to be unhappy because there is suffering in the world."

She smiled, leaning back in the chair, and a softness settled over her face. "I fell in love with him while he lectured me. There's something so grand about a man who knows how to live a fulfilled life, yet cares so deeply about others—you know?" she asked distantly, now looking at Stacey again as her thoughts returned to the present.

Stacey avoided her eyes and looked down at her coffee. "I can imagine," she said incidentally.

Maureen rose to refill her cup. "By the way," she said, "Eric has invited a group of children to the villa next Saturday. I'd like for you to help me with the plans, if you will."

"That should be fun," Stacey answered immediately, and lest her excitement be misunderstood, added quickly. "The children will love it."

"They always do," Maureen replied. "Eric does this several times a year. He enjoys it as much, if not more, than the children. You should see him at Christmastime."

"I wish I could, but I won't be here then." Stacey gasped, trying to cover the blush she felt rise to her cheeks. "Not even here long enough to get involved, and already I'm sad about leaving."

"Sometimes it doesn't take long, Stacey," Maureen correctly assessed, and Stacey wondered if they were referring to the same things.

"No, it doesn't take long," Stacey said suddenly, bringing her thoughts into focus, and remembering Fredrico. "I'd like to begin another sponsorship." Maureen smiled with pleasure. "Also, I'd like to buy Fredrico a pair of socks."

They laughed. "Be careful," Maureen warned. "Keeping that boy in socks could take more money than any of us has!"

With each passing day, Stacey found the work at the Field Office increasingly mind-boggling. The massive amount of paperwork and individual sponsorships were only a part of the services undertaken by the organization. There were institutions and educational centers to be maintained, including those for the blind, deaf, and handicapped. Provisions were made for day nurseries, elementary and secondary schools. Assistance was provided for vocational training centers and instruction in family planning.

"I had no idea so much was involved in the organization," Stacey said with wonder. "And so far I've become acquainted only with concepts. I haven't even seen it in action. There must be an enormous number of employees."

"Yes, and we couldn't begin to pay them what they're worth." Maureen's voice filled with pride and appreciation. "Then there are the volunteers who come during summer vacations—like you," she said smiling. "And those who help us out during their annual vacation—doctors, teachers, carpenters, office workers." She spread her hands as if there were too many to name. "And no gift is too small," she emphasized. "If one million persons give one dollar each, you can readily see what we'd have to work with."

"And all this is just the tangible, material side of it," Stacey said with awe.

Exactly," Maureen replied immediately. "To receive contributions and distribute them competently is our job, but not our purpose. This is not a mechanical organization, but a caring one. It's that personal involvement that makes this a real ministry."

On Friday morning, Stacey was able to be a part of that personal touch. Maureen handed her a box. Inside, was a cute little gold and white ball of fur that "meowed" faintly when she stroked its head.

"I want you to see this before we visit Fredrico," Maureen said after they climbed into the van filled with supplies and headed for the outskirts of Manila.

Soon they came upon women and children working in gardens. They waved as the van passed. Maureen stopped on a dirt road in a small barrio where women sat outside their houses, making hats and baskets. Older children played with smaller ones.

"This is an example of organized community planning," Maureen explained. "We offered the material and instruction. Now after a few years, they are almost entirely self-sufficient and productive individually and collectively."

Stacey pointed to a small white frame structure with a steeple. "And that's the ultimate goal?"

Maureen smiled. "We cannot, morally or legally, require anyone to accept the Christian religion as a prerequisite for receiving our help. But it is our aim for them to someday ask why we cared. Then we can reply that it is not out of pity, but because of our love for Jesus and obedience to His commands. Ours is not just giving, but giving in His name."

By that time, a crowd was gathering. A little girl about six years of age stood in front of the group and looked as if her eyes could not contain her excitement. She kept putting her hand over her mouth to stiffle some uncontrollable joy ready to burst forth.

"It's Luna's birthday," Maureen explained. "And she knows her sponsor will have sent something."

The little girl squealed with delight at the sight of the kitten. All the smiling women and other children "ooohed" and "aaaahed" and wanted to touch it with a finger.

Stacey observed as Maureen and Luna sat on a bench to write a letter to the sponsor. It was a painstaking job helping the little girl express her thoughts. Maureen wrote it down, then in large, bold print Luna copied each letter. Luna giggled, seeing the kitten lick its paws. She ended her letter by saying, "I love my kitten, and I love you."

Years ago Maila had written such letters, expressing her thanks to Stacey for a dress and a pair of shoes—a Christmas gift. She had drawn flowers and colored them with crayons. Looking at Luna, Stacey knew she would always be grateful to her sponsor. That was Maila's attitude, too. To herself, the Carlsons, and Eric.

The seemingly simple act with Luna took most of the morning. After they left the barrio, Maureen said, "We'll go to Fredrico's now." On the way, she related his case study. She didn't know all the details, for neither Fredrico's mother nor father would supply more than the barest facts necessary for the boy's sponsorship.

Fredrico had been too young to remember very much, but had spoken of their living up north and his father working in the rice fields. Then his little sister took sick. His mother begged for a doctor. The father brought a doctor who ran around the room, waving a sword and telling the *buso* to leave.

"Fredrico says his father insists that the *buso* killed his little girl and came to live inside himself, trying to steal his soul," Maureen said. "That's why they moved away, trying to escape the *buso*."

Stacey gasped in surprise. How strange, that Fredrico could be so dedicated and his father harbor such superstitions. "Does Fredrico really understand . . .?" she began, hardly knowing how to phrase the many questions crowding her mind.

"Definitely!" Maureen assured, and told her more about Fredrico. "The family moved here two years ago. His father began to make tuba, drinking more than he sold. Apparently laden with guilt, he becomes violent when drinking. Fredrico often hides in the trees."

Stacey could hardly reconcile in her mind the thought of that carefree child singing "Jesus Loves Me" and strumming on his ukelele with the knowledge that he was often forced to hide from a drunken father.

"Last year he came to the van one day in the village," Maureen was saying, "He said he had listened to the preacher from outside the church every chance he had. At first, he was attracted to the music. His father used to sing, and taught him to play the ukelele."

Maureen paused and cleared her throat. Stacey remembered that John had said how difficult it was to remain objective. After a moment, she continued.

"Fredrico told the preacher, who encouraged him to talk to me. He said that Jesus had come into his heart and he would grow up to tell others all about it. He told his father, who became angry. He didn't say what his father did, but there were bruises on his arms."

That was hard to believe. "Fredrico is such a bright child," Stacey mused. "I would expect his parents to be."

"Oh, his father is quite intelligent, even if uneducated," Maureen countered quickly. "That is why he can't tolerate Fredrico's talk of a forgiving Jesus. To accept that means to admit he was wrong about his former religion. Then it would have been his own ignorance and superstition that brought about the death of his little girl. He will not consciously do that. He fights the possibility of Fredrico's being right by drowning his conscience with tuba. The tuba has very likely damaged his brain by now. His wife says, 'Nico is a good man when he's not drinking. It's our little girl. He loved her so.'"

And they assigned Fredrico's case to me, Stacey thought ruefully. She dabbed at the moisture in her eyes.

Maureen stopped the van where a dirt road ended. They got out and began to walk along a path. "Something is wrong," she said, "or Fredrico would have met us by now."

In the midst of a patch of coconut palms, they came to a house built on piles and thatched with nipa. Propped against the entrance of the square dwelling no bigger than a large room was a portable ladder.

A woman in a dress too big for her thin frame stood barefoot in the yard, stirring a pot over an open fire.

She glanced up only briefly at Maureen's greeting, "Hello, Maria." She walked closer. "Where's Fredrico?"

Maria's furtive glance traveled toward the trees. "Playing," she said uncertainly.

"Where's Nico?"

Maria shook her head.

"Come on," Maureen said. Stacey followed up the shaky ladder and into a darkened room. When her eyes adjusted to the dimness, she saw a man lying on a padded mat against one wall.

"Nico," Maureen said loudly. "I want to talk to you."

The man didn't move.

"You must either talk to me, or I will get the authorities out here to find out about Fredrico."

He then rolled over and gave her a sullen look from dark brooding eyes, beneath thick brows. He sat up, his knees bent, reached over and picked up a brown cigarette and lit it, drew on it, and coughed.

He rested his forearms on his knees and leaned forward, looking at the floor. "What's this about Fredrico?" he asked finally.

"Were is he?"

"Out," he said. "Playing."

Maria had come in and was rolling up a smaller mat at the other side of the room.

"I want to see him," Maureen insisted.

"No," Nico replied flatly.

"Oh, all right," Maureen said staunchly. "Come on, Stacey. He doesn't want our help. We will inform the sponsor to stop payments and the authorities can deal with him concerning Fredrico." Turning on her heels, she walked toward the doorway. Stacey didn't know what to do but follow.

They stopped. Fredrico's head appeared at the doorway, then his body.

"Come over here, Fredrico," Maureen insisted gently, standing in the light from a window opening.

Fredrico looked at his father.

"Go on," Nico said roughly. He puffed on his cigarette, looking at Maureen, then Stacey.

The minute Fredrico stepped into the light, Stacey saw it. The red whelps across the side of his face. The barefoot boy, in short pants and no shirt, seemed frail and much younger than he had on Sunday.

Maureen knelt to examine the angry marks on Fredrico's face. She turned to Nico. Her voice was icy. "You've been drinking again, Nico."

"He fell."

Maureen looked at Fredrico who stared at the floor.

"Tell her," Nico said.

"It doesn't hurt now," Fredrico insisted.

"Where did he fall?"

"Outside. On a stick."

"A stick about the size of a man's hand, Nico?"

Nico raked his hair with his hand. Stacey feared he would burn his fingers, for the cigarette had burned down to a small stub. He swore and stood to stamp out the cigarette on the floor. His head almost touched the beams holding up the thatching. A raspy sound escaped his throat. "I can't blame him for loving you people more than he loves me. I can't blame him."

"No, daddy!" Fredrico ran to his father and grabbed him around the thighs, looking up at him pleadingly. "Don't say that, daddy! I love you! I know you don't mean to hurt me!"

The man seemed to break then. "I won't do it again." his voice choked on a hoarse sob and he clasped the child to him. "I wouldn't hurt my boy. He's all I got. I wouldn't hurt him."

Fredrico looked up and smiled at his daddy through tears that filled his eyes, than spilled down across the red, swollen stripes on his cheek.

Maureen cleared her throat and spoke softly. "The children have been invited to a party Saturday. We would like for Fredrico to go with us."

"Sure, if he wants to go."

"I do, daddy," Fredrico assured.

"Someone will come for him right after daybreak."

Maria followed them to the van. "Don't take away the money," she implored. "I won't let him hurt Fredrico again. I told Nico I will take the boy and go away if he lifts a hand to him."

"I'll give him one more chance," Maureen said, her voice grave. Maria's eyes filled with gratitude.

In the van Maureen stated what Stacey already knew. "We wouldn't take that sponsorship away from Fredrico. But it's the only weapon I have against Nico."

Some of Stacey's psychology studies came to mind. The class had read and discussed how some persons caused the very thing they most feared. Nico was afraid of losing Maria and Fredrico, as he had lost his little girl. Yet, his behavior was producing the opposite of what would draw them closer to him. Before now, the concept had been words in a book. She could not recall if the class had found a solution to such a state of mind.

Early Saturday morning, while children from the village loaded the bus, Stacey drove the van along the dirt road toward Fredrico's house. There was no sign of the small boy, but it was early. Perhaps he was still asleep. The sun was just topping over the palms.

When she rolled to a stop, Stacey could see that Maria wasn't in the yard. No ladder propped up against the entrance. She tried peering in, but it was useless. The floor came to the top of her head.

"Fredrico!" she called.

Her skin prickled when she heard a disgruntled sound. Then the ladder fell down so quickly she had to jump out of the way to avoid being struck. Nico, barefoot and shirtless, climbed down in wrinkled pants. Leaden eyes scanned the landscape. They widened in comprehension as they took in her sandals, designer jeans, and colorful shirt tied in a knot at her waistline.

"You're alone," he said flatly.

Stacey's instinct was to deny it. The fight-or-flight sensation traveled through her veins, while her mind acknowledged the truth that she could scream until doomsday without anyone hearing.

"I've come for Fredrico." Her voice was not nearly so authoritative as Maureen's.

He took a step nearer. She detected the odor of stale tuba. "Nobody's here but me," he said. She moved back.

"Maureen told you what we would do," she threatened.

"You're no good at this," he countered. "Neither of you would hurt my boy." A strange smile touched his lips. "He told me about you. All pretty and dressed up. Going to church. Singing. Working all summer without money." He snorted. "But you already got money. You never had a little girl, did you?" The harshness left his voice. "You never lost . . ."

He didn't finish. Stacey shook her head, and her face crumpled. She didn't want to run. Maybe she would feel better if he did hit her.

"But you love my boy," he said unexpectedly. "Better than I do."

"No," Stacey protested, facing the pain and frustration in his eyes. "Just differently. Maybe," she added uncertainly, "I can show you how."

"Sure," he sneered, as if she had claimed she could open up a bottle and produce a genie.

He paced several feet, then returned. "They went away last night. I don't know where. If you see them. . ." he began, then shook his head, turned, lifted his hand helplessly, climbed up the ladder, then disappeared into the darkened room.

Stacey returned to the field office, tears still streaking her cheeks. A busload of children waited impatiently. John and Maureen stood beside their car, eager to hear her news. "I can't go until I find out what happened to Fredrico." Seeing Maureen's glance at the bus of noisy children, she added quickly. "Oh, I know you have to go. Maybe I can get one of the office workers to go with me to Fredrico's later. He'll surely be back."

"Eric called last night before driving to the villa," John said. "He said something about Orlando's being in town, in case we needed anything. Just a minute." He disappeared into the building.

Several minutes passed before he returned. "I talked to Eric," he said. "Orlando will call him before leaving Manila this morning. He will have him stop by the office after completing his business in town." He glanced at his watch. "It will be at least two hours before the stores open."

Stacey nodded. "I'll call and let you know what's happening."

Watching as they drove out of sight, Stacey felt a keen disappointment. The first thought in her mind during the early morning was the party at the villa. Earlier, slipping into her swimsuit, she had remembered dancing blue eyes, cheeks dimpled with a smile, and a voice saying, "The commander likes the girl in the swimsuit very much."

Such thoughts must be laid aside, for of more pressing importance was a little boy whose disappointment went far deeper than her own. Wherever he was.

A short while later, the phone rang. It was Fredrico. A great weight lifted from her shoulders upon hearing his voice. After Nico had started drinking, his mother had taken him to the home of an old couple farther back in the palms. When they returned, Stacey had already gone. Fredrico went to the village and used the pastor's phone.

"Maybe we can make the party, after all, Fredrico," Stacey said excitedly. "You go back home, and I'll be there as soon as I can."

After Orlando arrived, Stacey called the villa and left a message with Francine that she and Fredrico would be coming with Orlando.

The momentary satisfaction that Orlando would be with her when she faced Nico soon vanished. It dawned on her that Orlando might be the one to fear. At least she knew Nico's problem. Orlando's suppressed feelings were dangerously near the surface.

"Sit up front," he demanded when she started to climb in back. "It will keep your hair from blowing so much."

So he had noticed the other time, but hadn't cared. She suspected he didn't care now. Anyway, it was arranged in a top knot with bangs over her forehead. After climbing in front, she decided to ignore his sullenness. "I appreciate your doing this, Orlando. Fredrico would have been so disappointed."

He did not verbalize the slight question she saw in his eyes when he glanced her way. He nodded once.

Before he could stop the van on the outskirts of Manila, Fredrico raced toward them, swinging his ukelele. Maria stood back and waved.

Stacey asked Orlando to stop at her apartment. She ran in for her box and cassettes, hoping that would occupy their time during the three hour drive to the villa.

Fredrico leaned over the front seat while Stacey showed him the controls. He tried every tape, asking questions about the music and the musicians.

Over an hour passed before he was satisfied enough to settle back against the seat, apparently fascinated with the various styles and types of music, from country, to classical.

Fredrico was completely absorbed in the music. His

music potential evidenced as he picked out melodies and played along on his ukelele. After a stop at a service station, he lay down in the seat and fell asleep.

Straightening in the seat, Stacey looked to her right for awhile, watching the landscape whiz by. Just as she leaned her head back against the seat, closing her eyes, Orlando asked, "Is the boy sleeping?"

Her eyes flew open. "Yes," she said, wondering if he had really spoken to her or if she had fallen asleep and imagined it.

"Is Maila at the villa?"

"No, she's working."

"Will she be there later?" he asked.

An uneasiness crept over Stacey. Why was he suddenly firing questions at her? "It wasn't mentioned. I mean . . . this is an outing for some of the children who are sponsored by the CF organization."

"She has been there many times with them."

"Yes, she used to work with the CF office."

The gaze he leveled at her lasted so long, Stacey wondered if he would run off the road. Then he returned his attention to his driving, asking, "You and she have become close since you arrived?"

"We've always been close—since we were teenagers. But yes, our relationship has grown. We are good friends."

"Then you confide in each other," he stated blandly.

Surely he couldn't expect her to betray a confidence, but she knew there was some underlying reason for this conversation. Her silence prodded him on. "Undoubtedly she has told you of her situation with Commander Farrington."

"Situation?"

"All right," he said, as if tired of hinting, ready to reveal what was on his mind. "That he is Maila's chance of a lifetime."

"Chance?" she replied, truly puzzled. "What kind of chance? Financially? Or are you talking about love?"

He glanced quickly toward her and back again. "Let's stop playing games, Miss Stamford. Could you love any man or would he have to possess certain qualities?"

"I'm sure you know the answer to that, Orlando," she replied stiffly.

"Don't you think Commander Farrington possesses qualities that a woman could love?" When she didn't answer, he continued. "We can assume he does. Then yes, that leaves the material side of things."

"Fine," Stacey said abruptly. "Then Maila has the possibilities of a very good future. That's wonderful," she said with finality. "I'm pleased for her."

"Yes," he said slowly. "You would be. Like you said, you two have become even closer now that you're here. Would you say that the admiration and respect she felt for you during the years is now transferred to the real you? The flesh and blood you?"

"Well . . . yes. It's only natural," she said defensively.

He nodded. "I knew it would be like that the minute I heard you were coming to the Philippines. It was in Tomas's attitude toward you, although your kindness to him was indirect. It was obvious in Maila's reactions on the way to the villa. The farm workers all talk about what a wonderful person you are."

"Believe me, Orlando. I haven't been seeking their approval. I . . ."

He interrupted her attempt at humility by saying harshly. "Let's not change the subject, Miss Stamford." She looked at him sharply. "What I'm saying is this. You have been very important to many people around here. Now you've materialized from words on

108

paper, and a monthly check. Don't you think you would have the same effect on Commander Farrington as on everyone else?"

Stacey gasped, then promptly closed her mouth. "The Carlsons, too," she reminded him. "And the reverse is true. I've admired them for years. Now that feeling is even stronger."

"I'm not talking about the Carlsons," he countered.

She drew in her breath. "I don't like the turn of this conversation, Orlando. Perhaps we should just end it."

"There's no need to become emotional, Miss Stamford," he replied with infuriating candor. "I'm just trying to be sure you realize the facts, since I witnessed a couple of disturbing incidents. Last Saturday night I came to pick Mother up, and walked out onto the courtyard. Maila was not there, but you and the Commander were in the pool. I shrugged it off. Then the following night, in the shadows at the side of the house . . ."

"Those weren't *incidents*, Orlando. Are you accusing me of something sordid?"

"Accusing? No. Just enlightening you. It's easy to see that Commander Farrington could become infatuated with a beautiful American woman." He said the words harshly. She knew they were not intended to be complimentary.

Her shoulders rose with indignation. Spying on them was one thing, but to make such unfounded implications . . . "Don't you think, Orlando," she asked pointedly, "that you're letting your personal feeings enter into this?"

"My personal feelings, Miss Stamford," he said bitingly, "were laid aside several years ago."

"Orlando, one cannot so easily lay aside—"

"Who said it was *easy*?" he interrupted. The muscle in his jaw tensed ominously.

"Well, let me assure you," she said uncomfortably. "I have no intentions—"

"Intentions, hah!" he scoffed. "I've been there. You think you can handle anything."

Neither said anything more for a long moment. Stacey told herself there was no need to be intimidated by Orlando. Apparently, he loved Maila. Or had at one time. He was still concerned with her welfare and future. No doubt he held some distorted view of American women. If his opinion were formed by American movies, that too, was understandable.

"You have a low opinion of me, don't you, Orlando?" she asked finally.

"On the contrary, Miss Stamford," came his immediate reply. "Commander Farrington is an honorable man. Being attracted to a woman is one thing. But only a fine person like yourself, would really pose a serious threat to Maila's happiness."

Before Stacey could remind him that she, too, had been concerned with Maila's happiness since the girl was eight years old, the van came to a stop at the villa's side gate. Eric, wearing shorts and an unbuttoned shirt, strode toward them.

Turning in the seat, her weight on her knees, Stacey leaned over the seat. "Fredrico!" she called excitedly. "Wake up, honey. We're here."

He woke with a start and sat up immediately, then a broad smile spread across his face when he saw Eric holding the door open for him. "Come on, son. We've been waiting for you," Eric said, but his dimpled smile was for Stacey. "Just in time for a swim."

"Oh, boy!" Fredrico exclaimed, then wilted slightly. "I don't do it very well."

"That's perfectly all right," Eric replied, tousling the boy's hair. "One swimming lesson coming up. And I volunteer Stacey to help me teach you."

Stacey turned in the seat, refusing to acknowledge

110

any sullen glance from Orlando that might dampen her spirits. Without looking at him, she opened the front door and jumped down.

"Sir!" Orlando called, before she could close it. He bent his head to look out at them. "Will you need me later to drive them back to Manila?"

"That won't be necessary," Eric replied, barely glancing at Orlando as he pushed the door closed. "It's not every day I have such a lovely guest." His eyes did not leave hers. "I may just keep her with me for a while."

It was not until she had responded with a delighted laugh that she realized Orlando might misinterpret Eric's banter. She opened her mouth to speak to him but he was already backing the van viciously. The engine growled as he rolled down the hill, stirring up clouds of dirt behind the spinning wheels.

CHAPTER 7

FREDRICO'S SWIMMING LESSONS turned out to be entertaining for everyone. Eventually he chopped through the water with a technique more reminiscent of a karate expert than a fish.

Luna had brought her kitten. Someone found a strip of wire to place over the top of its box so he wouldn't escape while she played in the pool. The activity delighted the children. Joe, the bus driver, along with CF office workers Kathy and Susan, divided them into groups who took turns swimming relays, touring the grounds for a lesson in flora, and walking out beyond the wall, along the road that wound through the coconut forest.

Eric brought out a replica of a ship he used to command. The young minds, alerted to the idea of high adventure quickly absorbed all Eric would tell them about the life of a naval commander.

He spoke solemnly of the necessity of military defense in order to protect their beautiful islands, the patriotic duty of citizens to preserve and insure their freedoms, the tranquil beauty of a starlit night reflected on the open sea, and the euphoria experienced in seeing the shores of one's homeland after a long voyage. He explained that his duties now were to train others to become captains of ships.

"Will they let us come and see the big ships?" asked one of the boys.

Eric smiled. "I think that could be arranged."

Stacey had the strong suspicion a new dream had just been born for many of the young boys sitting cross-legged at his feet.

As the evening sun streaked the sky with pink and gold, John and Maureen gathered the children around them at the far end of the pool to tell a Bible story. They concluded a rousing rendition of "Jesus Loves Me" accompanied by Fredrico's ukelele.

Joe, Kathy, and Susan helped Mrs. Molino and Francine set up a long table for the hamburger supper. Eric donned a chef's hat and insisted that Stacey assist him at the grill set up on the patio.

Hungry children, sitting around the poolside, consumed dozens of hamburgers. Luna's kitten lapped its milk, then fastidiously licked whiskers and paws.

When the time came to leave, each child received colorful paper bags filled with fruit, Francine's homemade cookies, a coloring book, and crayons. Each one, clinging to the handles, lifted a cherubic face and thanked Eric for the wonderful day.

Francine hugged Stacey and urged her to come again soon. She wished it didn't have to end. But Eric didn't keep her there. She rode back to Manila with John and Maureen. Fredrico rode the bus. He and his ukelele would be welcomed company on the return three-hour drive.

Stacey settled into another week at work, realizing her involvement with the children and their parents already far surpassed anything she would have accomplished with her foreign students at the university. The impact of her growing concern followed her even into the evenings. It could not be left behind, as if it were a letter typed, stamped, and sent off to be mailed. The needs of the people remained in her heart and mind.

Reading her impressions in her journal, she thought of Fredrico. When the summer ended, she wondered what would happen to the child and his family. Her mind wandered to Eric, who obviously loved children. Perhaps he could take a personal interest in the boy as he had in Maila so long ago. Even Nico might listen to Eric, since he was not a CF employee. She would talk to him about that.

When Eric called on Friday, saying he wanted to take her sightseeing the following day, she accepted. She would not insult Eric's offer of friendship by refusing his invitation. After all, they were both well aware of the situation, and she could not help adding to herself, *so is Orlando.* Last Sunday evening she sat with him, John and Maureen at church. She ate supper with the Carlsons on Tuesday. Thursday she and Maila went into Manila where they spent hours in the sari-sari stores. On Friday afternoon she and John sat in his office, drank coffee and discussed not only her work, but engaged in small talk.

Early Saturday morning, Stacey's sleepy eyes burned with anticipation as the glaze of dawn began to light the sky. "Dress casually," Eric had said. She wore khaki slacks and a red short-sleeved blouse and put her hair in a topknot, with feathered bangs.

When the Lincoln pulled up, Stacey hurried outside before Eric could reach her door. Wearing a blue and white knit shirt, open at the neck, he looked as fresh as the morning sky with its cotton-candy clouds. She inhaled deeply, savoring the cool air. His twinkling eyes flashed his admiration, but his words were for the package wrapped in blue and gold paper, tied with a big gold bow.

"What's this?" he asked.

"Later," she replied coyly. Eric looked at her curiously while holding open the car door. Propped on her knees, she leaned over the seat and put the package in back, then turned around and fastened her seat belt.

"Where to?" Stacey asked when Eric slid under the steering wheel and started the engine.

He shook his head, pulling out into the street. "You have secrets. I have secrets."

Stacey laughed. His answering grin dimpled his cheeks. It really didn't matter where they were going. She rolled her window down a little and felt the cool air on her face, ruffling her bangs.

The Lincoln sped along the quiet streets, across the Pasig River and onto the Escolta, the city's famous, now isolated, business thoroughfare. Along the north bank he slowed for a look at Malacanang, the president's palatial residence. "It's the Philippine White House," Eric said of the gleaming white rambling structure surrounded by Acacia trees adorning the lush green lawn.

"Breakfast?" Eric asked.

"Too early," Stacey replied. "I had coffee."

"Same here," he said. "We'll stop later for brunch."

They passed areas reflecting great prosperity, walled sections crumbling from earlier ravages of war. "Manila is a paradox. The modern and the ancient; the rich and the poor side by side," Eric said as they left the city behind, passed barrios composed of clusters of thatched huts, observed squatters' shacks, drove around crowded fishing villages hugging crystal-clear waters, and sped toward mountains looming mysteriously into the sky.

"John is so right," Stacey began, feeling a sudden release of tension. "He has stressed the need for us to get away from our work, relax, have fun, and forget the problems. He says it helps to keep things in perspective."

"I certainly agree," Eric concurred. "That's how I feel about the villa. Although the manual labor on the farm is done by others, the place is a big responsibility and the livelihood of many persons depends on decisions that are ultimately mine. Yet, it's relaxing much of the time, and a needed diversion from my week at the base."

"Do you plan to stay here for the duration of your military career?" Stacey asked.

"Depends upon what the future holds," he said, pausing to look out at the lake on their right, then continued the ascent along the mountainous road. "I've had my day of training in the States, service in a European country, adventure on the high seas, and now land duty on a tropical island."

"Yours sounds like a very exciting life," Stacey observed wistfully.

"The advantages have far outweighed the disadvantages," he agreed. "Especially for a daring, young bachelor. But my outlook has changed as I've grown older. My personal involvement with the people here is my major reason for choosing to stay in the Philippines. There's the farm, the villa, the Carlsons, the children," he glanced her way and smiled. "And Maila."

Stacey studied the high mountains that were coming into view. What more could one want than a place of service, friends, a place to relax, someone to love? "You're fortunate, Eric. To be able to live or work almost anywhere you like."

"Yes, in that respect, I am," he said. "And I'm fortunate to have a father who is a retired admiral and a brother who teaches at Annapolis." They exchanged a smile. "Connections help," he said and quickly added, "However, one is not put in command of a ship because of one's connections."

"Let's hope not," Stacey retorted.

"But there are those," he said in a more jovial tone, "who pity me. They feel the ideal life is settling down with a wife and children."

"And what do you think?" Stacey prodded.

"I'm not averse to that idea," he assured, grinning. "My twenty-year retirement is just seven years away. It has crossed my mind to transfer back to the States and teach at Annapolis. I could sell the farm and keep the villa. It might also be a valuable source of income as rental property for military personnel coming to the Philippines for duty at Subic Bay."

"After so many years here, Eric, do you think you'd be happy in the States?"

"With a family of my own, yes. Although there is a great sense of pride and desire for freedom here in the islands, and a growing feeling of nationalism, I'm not sure my own children would consider this their country. And it isn't home for me. The U.S.A. is home. I want my children to grow up with pride, patriotism, and a love for their country. Christian values. All that can be taught regardless of where I am, of course, but environment is important, and I don't want to deprive them of growing up in the greatest nation in the world with the feeling of optimism that is inevitably a part of the American spirit."

But the Philippines is home for Maila. How would she feel about leaving her country? Stacey wondered.

"Unless," he said suddenly, breaking her reverie, "my wife might object and insist I be stationed in some exotic port so she could lead the adventurous life!"

Stacey laughed. "I'm sure a life with you anywhere would be adventurous, Eric." she said and he lifted an eyebrow, glancing her way. "I mean, your reasons of wanting to rear your children in the States are certainly valid." She remembered Maila couldn't imagine her existence without him. "I'm sure your wife would be happy with you, wherever you lived."

"She would have to be," he answered quickly. "And vice-versa. The last thing I need is a one-sided relationship. My wife will have to love me as much as I love her, and we must share basic values. There must be a mutual caring, and a mutual respect."

Stacey looked out at the steep, pine-covered mountains, realizing how the minutes and miles were speeding by. That mutuality had been absent in her relationship with Randy. Or perhaps their basic values were different. Then she felt a hand on hers.

"You're miles away," Eric said softly.

"I'm sorry," she said and looked down again.

"Don't be," he said giving her hand a squeeze before returning his to the wheel. "Want to talk about it?"

"There's nothing to say."

"All right. Then I'll continue with the many heartaches of Eric Farrington. Unless you prefer to pass the time discussing a more interesting subject."

"I can't think of a more interesting subject," she replied, and laughed as if she were joking.

He began with early childhood and how, every time he fell in love, his family moved to another naval base. "The worst time was in high school when I had to leave my sweetheart. That was devastating and I promised to return so we could sail off into the sunset together." He shook his head. "But my fickle heart found another girl at Annapolis." He laughed lightly. "Then her fickle heart found another guy."

"Is that what happened with Ingrid?" she asked, curious.

"Not exactly," he replied thoughtfully. "After Annapolis, I was stationed in Germany. We discussed marriage. I didn't realize it at the time, but Ingrid didn't really have first place in my life. The Navy did. Commanding a ship at sea was a dream that had to be fulfilled." He looked over at Stacey and smiled. "Nor was Ingrid's commitment to me as great as she had thought. We were in love perhaps, but not ready for marriage."

"Was she beautiful?"

"Oh, yes," he said a reminiscent look on his face. "Georgous blond, with big green eyes." He grinned.

"You seem to have survived it all right."

"Sometimes it takes distance to put things into perspective. I asked for and received my transfer to the Philippines, and eventually came to the conclusion that marriage to Ingrid would have been a mistake."

Stacey hadn't realized Eric was slowing the car until he pulled over to the side of the road and parked beside a tree-lined sidewalk. He switched off the engine, turned in the seat, his arm spread across the back, his fingers within inches of her shoulder.

"To me, Stacey, marriage has taken on a far deeper significance since my infatuation with Ingrid. Then, it was based on surface qualities mainly, the good times we could have together. I still want those things in a woman, but I want much more. For marriage, we must be compatible in wanting to share our lives with others, not just ourselves."

Maila had those qualities, she was thinking. Outer beauty and a caring heart. Eric's were noble aspirations and well within his reach. But when he said "infatuated" her memory recalled Orlando's words, "Commander Farrington could become infatuated with a beautiful American woman like you." As Orlando implied, and now Eric, infatuation left something to be desired in a relationship.

Trying to rid herself of the uncomfortable feeling, she looked around. "Oh, the present," she said suddenly. "You may open it now."

He reached for the package.

Stacey unfastened her seat belt and turned toward him to watch his response as he removed the bow, lifted the top, unfolded the white tissue, and lifted the brass bell, with an ornately carved Spanish design handle. His parted lips and twinkling eyes expressed his delight as he held the bell at eye level, shook it, and a musical tone sounded in their ears.

"It's for the villa," she said. "A dinner bell."

He jiggled it again. "Now we won't have to summon our guests with a spoon clanging against a glass." They laughed. He replaced the bell in its bed of white tissue. "It's wonderful, Stacey. But when I talked to you about guests giving presents, I wasn't . . ."

"Now Eric," she chided, "You lectured me on the art of receiving gracefully. Now you can demonstrate."

He nodded as he replaced the lid and returned the box to the back seat. When he turned again, his fingers did touch her shoulders, feeling almost like a caress. "Thank you, Stacey," he said softly. "You're very thoughtful."

She lifted a hand and made the familiar gesture at her ear. How foolish. Her hair was in a topknot.

"Where are we?" she managed to say, forcing her eyes away from his intent gaze, and peered past him out the window.

"Come on," he said. "I'll show you."

"This is Baguio," Eric said as they walked along the tree-lined streets in the quaint mountain resort. "It was designed by an American architect back in the early 1900s."

Stacey inhaled deeply. "I smell strawberries," then added, "and pine."

Eric smiled. "This is called the 'City of the Pines.' Many people smell gold,"he added, not entirely joking. "Baguio is right in the midst of the gold-mining region of the Philippines."

They walked around a corner and down a side street with many little shops, displaying native handicrafts.

"Let's go in here," he said, coming to a shop where baskets and hats were displayed in the windows. They laughed as he plopped hat after hat on her head, then decided on a floppy one that drooped over part of her face. "We'll take it," Eric said.

Further down the street they entered a restaurant with tables beneath the palms. While they waited for a table, Eric explained. "It's merienda time, somewhat like the American coffee break. The Filipinos have continued the Spanish custom of a mid-morning snack."

After they were seated at a small round table, Stacey held her hat on her lap. They ate scrambled eggs and crunchy fried shrimp that Eric called 'kropek.' Over a second cup of coffee, Stacey leaned forward and sighed contentedly. "This is wonderful, Eric. Thank you for such a lovely time."

She was reluctant to leave Baguio, but Eric made the point when he walked over to put her hat on her head. They drove past the Philippine Military Academy, golf courses, elegant hotels, lovely summer homes of wealthy Filipinos, and out to the hot springs.

"You've heard of the boondocks?" Eric asked as they headed in the direction of the Sierra Madre mountains.

"For ages," she laughed. "But I've never been sure what it meant."

"It's military slang for back country, mountain country, or someplace far from civilization. The word here is *bundok*."

121

"Are you trying to tell me something, Eric?" Stacey asked, looking out at the mountain forests.

He laughed at her skepticism. "This may seem uncivilized in comparison with Baguio, Manila, or America. It's Igorot country. There are many groups called by different names. The Ifugaos, Bontoks and Naboloi have communities on the mountainsides. Their dwellings are built on stone piles with thickly thatched roofs to help protect against torrential rains."

Stacey looked up at the sky and he added with a laugh. "Although the rains do occur suddenly, I don't think we have to worry about it today."

Stacey gasped. "What is *that*, Eric?" They were surrounded by mountains, like green stairsteps climbing to the sky.

"Ifugao rice terraces," he explained. "This should be called one of the wonders of the world. One mustn't come to the Philippines without seeing them. We're told that it has taken the Ifugaos two thousand years to make the rice terraces, and their ancestors completed them about a thousand years ago. Fifty-foot rock walls were constructed to hold the paddy fields."

"It's incredible!" Stacey exclaimed. "And as impossible to comprehend as the Egyptian pyramids. How do they get to the top?"

"They climb straight up. It's a mark of a man to conquer the mountain. They take pride in it. Farther north," he said, driving slowly along the mountain road so Stacey could get a good look at the terraces that reached to the summit of the mountains, "are the Ilongots. You may have read about them. A few years ago some were discovered who were reported to still be using iron age tools."

"Seems I read something about it," Stacey recalled.

"Rumor has it that the men hunt for heads."

She looked at Eric quickly to see if this were another joke. "Not really," she protested.

"Don't worry. That's a thing of the past," he said confidently and she felt he was enjoying her momentary discomfort. "Although you *will* occasionally see a sign warning tourists that it is head-hunting season again. Several years ago they had a hunt out for a particular missionary's wife. You see," he glanced toward her, "their most highly prized trophy is a white female's head."

"Are you sure it's a thing of the past?" Stacey asked uneasily.

He shrugged. "All I know is hearsay, Stacey. Put the hat on, perhaps they won't notice how pretty yours is."

"I wouldn't want to chance it," she said emphatically.

"If you will notice, we're heading back down the mountains."

That was some small comfort, but she would feel better when they were at the foot of the mountain.

"The missionaries have penetrated almost all of the jungles making converts and eliminating the head-hunting custom." There was a long pause before he made another remark calculated to raise the chill bumps on her flesh. "I've heard the natives have a ceremonial dance, and play a guitar-like instrument with strings made from human hair. Then the next night, they might have a prayer meeting."

Stacey rolled her eyes, thinking Sundays were probably the prayer meeting days. "Saturday doesn't seem like a very good day for white females in this area," she quipped. She laughed with him but kept a careful watch for a man who might swoop down on them, swinging on a rope. All she saw, however, was an occasional hut, with women sitting peacefully outside, weaving colorful material beneath the shade of a thatched overhang.

"There are several places we could stop for our mid-afternoon lunch, but I have a hunch you wouldn't like any of them as well as the restaurant in Baguio," Eric surmised correctly, and she smiled at him. "That will take at least a couple of hours. Why don't you tell me about Randy now."

"There's nothing to tell," Stacey replied immediately and knew her reply was too quick, yet there was truth in it. Randy's memory had dimmed in the light of her work and activity in the Philippines. More than once, she thought how fortunate Maila and Maureen were to have men in their lives who shared their concern for humanity.

Eric said nothing more, and Stacey knew he wouldn't pressure her. He had offered to be a sounding board if she needed one and had even eased the way for her by telling her about the girls he had loved in his younger days. "What I mean, Eric," she began again, "is that I'm not heartbroken."

Once she started, the words seemed to tumble out. Her tempestuous two-year relationship with Randy, her staking everything on the handsome prof, her walking in on him with another girl in a little restaurant that was supposed to be their own private, special place.

"His seeing someone else is not what bothers me," Stacey admitted. "I understand that relationships grow or deteriorate. It's his dishonesty that I can't accept."

"Could it be that they were just friends, Stacey?"

She shook her head. "That's part of the problem. He assured me I was the only woman in his life, and pressed me for a decision concerning marriage. After I confronted him about the girl in the restaurant, he passed her off as a 'temporary distraction.' I think I hurt for her as much as for myself. It's just that . . ."

Stacey inhaled deeply, not finishing her thought.

"Just *what*, Stacey," Eric probed, his voice gentle.

"I don't know exactly. It did something to my sense of trust in Randy. In everyone I suppose. I know there are people who are trustworthy. But I can't naïvely or innocently trust again."

"Those are painful lessons we all learn eventually, Stacey," he said. "Sometimes we even surprise ourselves when we discover perhaps we cannot be trusted implicitly. None of us is above temptation, you know."

"I realize that," Stacey agreed. "And people can't always control how they feel about another person. Before marriage is the time to find out those things. But Randy insisted he was certain that we were meant for each other. After I broke off with him, he admitted there had been several women in his life while he was telling me I was the only one. He said they meant nothing. I don't think the other women would like that description."

"Apparently he wants you back, Stacey," he said, referring pointedly to the letter she received.

Stacey recalled that he had seen Randy's return address on the envelope that Maureen had given her. She nodded. "That's what he says."

Eric maneuvered the car around a steep curve. "Do you think you can forgive him?"

"I already have," she answered truthfully. "I can understand that Randy is not as mature as I had thought, and that he's not ready for marriage, by my definition. I'm terribly disappointed, and it hurts. But no, I don't want to marry Randy. Not now, not ever."

The thoughtful expression remained on Eric's face for quite a while before he spoke. "Stacey, I can understand some of what you're feeling," he said. "Ingrid found someone else even before I left Germany. A part of me knew we weren't meant to be life companions, yet another part of me found her a hard habit to break. People become a part of your life. For a while I was definitely on the rebound, and didn't have the retrospective wisdom I now possess.''

He grinned. She knew he was joking, and yet believed the passing of time did bring objectivity. ''Later,'' he said, ''I discovered that was not the end of my relationships with women. Each heartache prepares us for that very special someone. For me it has brought a greater appreciation for the love that a woman may offer me, or that I may offer her. But I suppose those are things you'll have to discover for yourself.''

Stacey thought about his implication that there were other kinds of relationships than those ending in marriage. Of course she was aware of the relaxed standards of American culture. Was it true in the Philippines, as well? Well, not for her. When dating, she always wondered if the man were the life's companion ordained by God. Perhaps Eric was referring to friendship.

She almost panicked when she realized she wanted to hear Eric say he loved Maila. She *needed* to hear it. Some indication. Something to force her wayward mind to accept the friendship he offered, without her heart taking off in such impossible directions. She should not be thinking how well they got along, how much she enjoyed being with him, how handsome, how very special . . . Her thoughts stopped and veered suddenly. Those were the kinds of things Maila had said about Orlando. And where had that relationship ended? Heartache . . . disillusionment . . . seven years of Orlando's pining away for some-one he couldn't have.

Attempting to dispel the undesirable thoughts, Stacey said suddenly, ''Tell me about your work at the base, Eric.'' Soon, she felt at ease with him again as they talked about his lifestyle, then hers in Carbondale.

Her errant thoughts were left behind, just as they left behind the winding roads shaded by a forest of trees and entered the valley of brilliant mid-afternoon sunshine. As the warmth invaded the car, Stacey rolled down the window to welcome a piney fragrance.

"That's our table," Eric said to the waitress at the restaurant in Baguio, as if he were serious. "Do you think we could sit there?"

"Of course," she said sweetly, smiling from one to the other as if they were newlyweds.

Then he grinned at her while the waitress put their menus in front of them. Before he opened it, he asked, "Would you like to try the lumpia?"

"Sure," she said immediately.

He lifted an eyebrow. "Do you know what it is?"

"No, but I'm game."

"Even if it's turtle eggs and snails?"

The corners of her mouth turned down and she shook her head.

"It's pork, shrimp, coconut pith, and vegetables, wrapped in leaves, with the most delicious brown sauce you've ever tasted."

"You're been here before," Stacey observed.

Eric opened the menu, as if looking it over. Then he glanced across at her. "I've never brought anyone here twice in one day before."

Stacey's heart leapt and she laughed aloud to cover her own foolishness. That ridiculous statement meant exactly nothing, yet when he said it and his eyes twinkled across at her, it seemed to hold some special meaning. It must be the mid-afternoon sun, she thought. She allowed herself to wonder briefly whom he had brought here, and when, and why.

"Lumpia it is," she said suddenly. She opened her

127

menu. "And *this*," she said after careful scrutiny, pointing out a dish.

"Good enough," he said of her choice of a fruit plate consisting of tondan, a sweet banana, figs, melon, and pineapple.

After coffee they headed back to Manila, and Stacey told Eric about Fredrico and his family.

"If Nico is willing to try," Eric said after hearing the story, "I can give him a job on the farm. Of course it would involve moving."

Stacey choked back tears of joy. This was almost more than she could have hoped for. She reminded herself to be patient. It would take time to convince Nico. But it was a very real hope.

"Anytime you want my help, Stacey," he said softly, "all you have to do is ask."

She bit her lip and the wetness spilled over onto her cheeks.

When they reached her apartment and Eric thanked her again for the bell, and she thanked him for the tour, she thought about Orlando's having nothing to fear about Commander Farrington. The outing had been a lovely one. Nothing disastrous had happened. Eric was a gentleman, and a friend. It was over.

Then he said, "I'm not ready for the evening to end just yet, Stacey. Suppose I come back in a couple of hours, and we watch the sun set over Manila Bay."

CHAPTER 8

STACEY SHOWERED AND SHAMPOOED. dressed in a crinkle gauze float with a low-cut rounded neckline and puffs of sleeves barely covering her shoulders. The thin material, a subdued multi-colored print on a natural background, fell in soft folds to her knees. She blow-dried her hair, curled it under and let it hang to her shoulders, tucked one side behind an ear and fastened in gold earrings. A light application of make-up completed the effect. She stepped into bone-colored high-heeled sandals and turned to appraise herself. The movement of the soft material gave her a feminine, graceful, and free feeling.

I've never dressed up for a sunset before, Stacey said to herself, while spraying perfume behind her ears, then on her wrists.

Eric had changed, too, she noted when he appeared later. The ivory hue of his sports shirt contrasted with the heightened bronze of his tanned skin.

"You're very beautiful tonight," he said, not taking his eyes from the road when he pulled out onto the street.

It seemed that time stood still between the moment when she uttered a soft "thank you" and when they stood on the Luneta esplanade, in the tropical dusk. She had never seen anything like it. Throngs of people lined the shore, staring at the flaming sunset, a glorious ball of orange fire sending streaks of gold shimmering on the bay, turning the palms to shadows and the distant mountains to silhouettes.

"You are a golden girl," Eric said, bringing Stacey to the awareness that the scene was not the only enthralling experience on the beach. His arm moved to her shoulders and hers naturally sought his waist. Turning slightly, she looked up at him and it occurred to her that King Midas had extended his magic touch, turning the whole world to gold.

His face was so close she felt the breath that whispered the words, watched his tongue moisten his lips, felt the rise of his chest, saw his golden eyes as they found her parted lips.

The statement was as plain as if it had been spoken audibly, perhaps plainer. It said he wanted to be more than her friend. Much more. And Stacey knew she could no longer delude herself. It was not Midas and his magic, but a very real and frightening emotion that had sprung to life between them.

Like a shadow, her eyelids flickered to shut out the sudden pain. When she opened them the sky looked the same. That brief encounter couldn't have lasted over an instant, a second, a minute fraction of time, and yet . . . something had changed.

As the sun sank lower, the distinct horizon disappeared, leaving behind subdued shades of gray. Life was like that, she thought. There had been a time when she was positive of dangers, deep waters, dark places to avoid. Now they seemed to mingle together—like the sky, the bay, and the mountains.

For the first time in her life she felt a great

incompleteness, a vacuum. Her life had been filled with her faith, friends, family, job, activities, personal interests, boyfriends. It was as if Eric had looked into the future and predicted her needs when he said that each lost love is preparation for a greater one. She felt that now, a longing for a love that was deeper, stronger, more fulfilling than any she had yet experienced.

The crowd began to drift away from the shoreline, talking in low tones as if evaluating the experience of the dying sun. A sudden chill invaded her heart when Eric moved his arm away, but the warmth returned when he took her hand and their fingers entwined. They walked that way, hands swinging, arms touching, footsteps slowly seeking a destination.

They came to a stand of palms. He led her beneath one of them, away from the searching beams of a silver moon on the rise.

Lifting her hand to Eric's chest, she felt the rhythmic beating, imitating that of her own heart. She sensed again the control that must come from his years of military discipline, but his eyes betrayed his feelings. One of his hands was on the palm tree, bracing himself away from her. The other hand slowly sought the nape of her neck and entwined in her hair. The gentle pressure drew her head back and she lifted her face to his. He was giving her every opportunity to back away, call a halt, for his eyes watched her carefully, as if knowing she was deciding, thinking, and more than that, feeling.

Slowly, deliberately, still seeking her submission or retreat, his lips touched her face, gently, like a breath skimming across her cheeks, making a path down her neck.

The warm gentle waves that caressed the shore seemed to be caressing her senses, sweeping over her as ebb and tide of emotion began to erase all reason, replacing it with the sweet, wonderful feeling of belonging she experienced in Eric's arms, now enfolding her, drawing her closer to himself.

"Stacey," he whispered against her ear. "I've wanted to hold you in my arms since I first set eyes on you." He began the path back toward her lips, pausing briefly at the corner of her mouth.

Her lips parted with the breath of expectancy. Both her hands moved from his chest and toward his neck to embrace him and her eyes closed. The last thing she wanted now was to remember Orlando's warnings. Or perhaps it was her own conflicting emotions tearing at her heart. Her own conscience seemed to scream that she was a threat—a threat to her own dear friend, whose face swam before her momentarily, first the child, with sad, soulful eyes pleading for survival, then the young woman with trusting eyes of friendship.

Only her desperate cry stood between her and the wonderful, terrible thing she had almost done.

"No!"

Like stone, he stood. The only movement was the rise of his chest as he inhaled deeply of the night air, and held it.

"I'm so sorry," she said brokenly, turning in his arms and propping her forearm against the tree, leaning her head against it. "Please forgive me."

But she knew it wouldn't be that simple. He must wonder what kind of game she played with him. Never before had she walked into such a situation. She had even allowed, really encouraged, him to say those beautiful words to her that he must now be regretting.

A strange stillness settled on the night, and a long moment passed before he said, "Let's go back." His words weren't harsh; just distant and final.

Stacey fell in step beside him, knowing there was

no way they could recapture their former easy comaraderie. Nor could they move forward.

They reached the car and rode in silence. He deserved an explanation. But what to say, and how to say it, she didn't know.

"Eric, could we talk, please?" Stacey asked when he pulled the car to a stop in front of her apartment.

His voice was as serious as his face, void of dimples and with eyes that did not dance. "There's no need for a long discussion, Stacey. I can understand if you need to sort out your feelings for Randy before you're ready for another relationship."

Stacey could no longer look at him and turned her face away. How incredible that only a short while ago the world was aglow with a golden sky. But the day had died, leaving behind only darkness, a sliver of a moon beginning to rise from behind a distant mountain. That glow she had felt in Eric's arms must also fade and die.

Unable to find expression for her conflicting emotions she reached for the door handle but paused when he spoke again.

"Perhaps you feel there is no place in your life for me, Stacey. I've already told you I'm not interested in a one-sided relationship. We can just say tonight was my mistake, and I promise it won't happen again. All you need to do is tell me you don't want anything more than friendship from me."

She faced him then, knowing he would not pursue her for a minute if he thought she didn't care. And knowing too, she could not encourage him. With bent head and eyelids lowered, a sob escaped her throat. "I can't honestly say that, Eric."

The light from the rising moon filtered through the windshield onto her face. Eric lifted her chin with his fingers and wiped away the moisture that lay like silver spangles on her cheeks.

"Let's go inside," he said gently.

Stacey turned on a lamp in the living room, then they went into the kitchen where she switched on the overhead light and put coffee on to perk, still uncertain as to how to begin.

Turning from the countertop, she walked to the table and held on to the back of a chair, then looked across at Eric, leaning against the door casing, his hands in his pockets, waiting.

"It shouldn't be so hard to say, Eric," she began hesitantly.

He walked over to the table then, and held onto a chair opposite her. "If you must, then just say it, Stacey. But don't feel you have to make any confessions to me. If I moved too quickly it's because I'm aware of how little time we have. Almost half of your eight weeks at the center is over, and I must spend some weekends at the villa. There isn't much time for us. But if I'm rushing you . . ."

"Oh, Eric," she said, contrition in her voice. "I don't mean to make you feel guilty. You've done nothing out of line. At least, not any more than I've allowed." She looked down at the table then, avoiding his searching eyes.

"Then what, Stacey?" his voice pleaded. "Is it Randy? You're not sure? It's too soon?"

"I suppose it's Randy, in a way," she admitted. "My situation with him has made me realize a few things. I keep hearing him say that the other women meant nothing to him. They were temporary distractions. I . . . don't want to be that to anyone."

"Stacey," he said with irony as he walked around the table, put his hands on her shoulders, turning her to face him. "Surely you don't think I take you, or your feelings lightly."

"I don't think you're like that, Eric. But you did speak of different kinds of relationships, and I'm well

134

aware there are many. Some of my own friends have ideas opposed to mine. Some throw caution to the wind because they don't know what tomorrow holds, and they want their fun today.''

She could not bear the intensity of his gaze, so she focused on the first button that was fastened on his shirt. "Those are tempting concepts, Eric. But I don't want to be a summer fling for someone. I want to be more than that to a man, and I want him to be more to me.''

Stacey was grateful for the things she had learned from the bitter experience with Randy. She had learned she wanted a man she could trust, someone who wanted a mutual commitment, a shared faith in God, a willingness to work with a relationship. Those were things Maila would have with Eric, if some other woman did not come between them.

"I didn't mean to pressure you, Stacey. I just wanted to let you know how I feel.''

With his face so close and his hands on her shoulders, there was nothing to do but show her own feelings, far deeper than she wanted to admit to herself. She moved away, hugging her arms to herself, feeling a chill in the room. "Regardless of how you and I might feel about each other,'' she stammered "there is Maila to consider. We can't hurt her this way. I cannot.''

The silence was so long, Stacey wondered if he would respond to her words. Her eyes pleaded for his understanding, and suddenly knew she did not need to plead, for assent was in his eyes. "You're right, of course,'' he said. "We must never hurt Maila. But Stacey . . . how would this hurt her?''

Stacey was momentarily stunned. Then she realized that Eric certainly had women friends during the years Maila was growing up. Perhaps that casual kind of relationship was still part of his lifestyle. Or was he playing the kind of games that Randy had played? "Eric," she said slowly, "The way she loves you."

A kind of incredulous shock seemed to register on his face. He inhaled deeply. "Is . . . the coffee ready?" he asked.

Stacey passed him and took cups from the cupboard. When she brought the filled cups to the table, he had walked into the living room, his back turned. She got cream and spoons, then sat heavily at the table. After a long time he returned, pulled out a chair and sat down. He glanced at her, then put cream in his coffee and stirred thoughtfully.

"What do you mean?" he asked finally. "The *way* she loves me?"

"Well, she's expecting to marry you and . . ."

"Did she say I had asked her to marry me?" Eric asked, as if astounded.

Stacey felt uneasy. "Not in so many words. But she expects it. She says her family expects it. I know Orlando does because he warned me that . . ." She hesitated, feeling self-conscious, but determined that Eric not think she had made up such tales, or had connived to bring out his feelings for her. "He warned that my being an American et cetera, could become a . . . well, distraction for you, and cause irreparable damage between you and Maila."

"Orlando told you that?"

"Yes."

"Why?"

"Eric, I feel I'm betraying confidences now. I can't do that."

He stroked his chin thoughtfully and stared at her so long she had to look down at her steaming coffee. She did not like this, but it had to be faced.

"He's certainly right about your being a distraction, Stacey. From the moment I first saw you." He paused and Stacey said nothing. Finally he continued. "If

136

Maila expects to marry me, then irreparable damage could be done. There are things here I'm beginning to realize about many people that have seemed a mystery. And one of those is Orlando."

"Eric, please understand that I mustn't be a source of contention between you and Orlando. He mustn't know I even mentioned him." A sob was in her throat. "I can't stay in the Philippines and be a troublemaker."

"You're not, Stacey," he assured quickly. "On the contrary you've cleared up a number of things for me. You probably won't believe this, but I've never made any kind of personal commitment to Maila."

"Surely, Eric," she said slowly, "you know how she loves you."

"Of course," he replied quickly, then hesitated slightly before adding, "it's only natural, when you consider our relationship since she was fourteen. That's ten years, Stacey, that I have been the giver; she, the recipient. But only this moment am I beginning to comprehend the extent of it. Strange, how we can overlook something that is so close, so obvious," he mused.

"Yes, and for you and me to be more than friends would be like . . ." she struggled for words, then added, "like taking away Luna's kitten, or . . . Fredrico's ukelele . . . or even . . . Nico's little daughter."

"I know how much she has loved you, too, Stacey. And I, have put her through school, remembered her on special occasions, even helped other members of her family."

Stacey lifted her coffee cup to her lips and watched Eric over the rim of it. He seemed to be reminding himself of facts he knew well, but had never consciously thought about before, as he stared at a distant wall.

137

Then his eyes found hers again. "The Filipinos are basically Oriental, Stacey, in their sense of obligation to family members and others who do them a kindness. I haven't given this much thought, because I think like an American. I expect Maila to be appreciative, perhaps call me Dad . . ." He started to laugh, then regarded her soberly. "She's your age, isn't she?"

Stacey nodded.

In apparent frustration, he ran his fingers through his hair, disrupting his curls. "Please forgive me for drawing you into this strange kind of triangle, Stacey. Try to believe it wasn't intentional. You have opened my eyes to something I've refused to see."

"Forgive me, Eric," she countered. "Apparently you didn't realize. But I knew. I was told. I was warned. I am the offender."

He rose from his chair and came to sit beside her, then reached for her hands.

"You have not offended me," he protested, "I'm flattered, honored really, that you have spent time with me. But I am a little put out with you." Her questioning eyes met his. "I used all my charm, Stacey, tried to make you fall for me, but you were so resistent. I was begining to have a complex . . ."

"Eric," she said, and couldn't help but laugh.

"That's better," he said, his cheeks dimpling and his blue eyes twinkling. "Things aren't so terrible, are they?"

Stacey shook her head and looked at her hands captured in his strong ones. The feelings she had for Eric made those for Randy dim in comparison. She was left with an aching heart, a vision of love that could never be. But no, it was not so terrible as if she and Eric acted on their feelings.

"Look at me," he said, and she did. "You were right that we can't afford to hurt Maila. She's not prepared to be disappointed by the Americans who have given her a chance in life. I do love her and care about her feelings. From the time you were fourteen you've had a way about you that has forced me to become a better man than I might have been. I shall try to handle this situation with honor. Again, thank you."

Stacey's eyes closed when he leaned forward, whispered, "unfinished business," and caressed her lips with his own. Almost as soon as they touched, he squeezed her hands, moved away and stood. "Good night, Stacey. When I come to you again, and I will, it will be without any misunderstandings."

Stacey was grateful for her growing relationship with Fredrico. After church on Sunday morning she asked his parents about taking him to a matinee the following Saturday. Even Nico was receptive to the idea. Maria walked with her to the Carlsons' car and said that Nico was trying not to drink so much.

Stacey smiled to herself. At least, she could be happy there was some progress with Fredrico's family. The boy had accepted her friendship and needed to talk with her about plans for his life, so foreign to his present lifestyle. She was certain Eric would not forget their conversation and would help if needed after she left the Philippines. She needed to have this feeling of being useful and helpful to someone, that her life was counting for something.

"You will have lunch with us, won't you, Stacey?" Maureen asked as they neared their home.

She was about to consent, wanting to keep herself occupied and talk about her work with the Carlsons, when John added, "We knew Eric stayed in town this weekend and asked him to lunch, but he called this morning to say he couldn't make it."

He was afraid I'd be there, she thought and her

139

spirits plummeted, although she knew he was doing the right thing. Perhaps the Carlsons knew about their sightseeing trip. She did not feel like discussing it. "Thanks, but I'll pass on lunch today."

"We'll pick you up later for church then," Maureen offered.

Stacey declined that offer too, using the excuse of catching up on her journal entries. "Otherwise," she said, trying to keep her voice light, "I'll never earn my master's." It was a valid excuse, she told herself, for she needed that sense of accomplishment to take back to the States with her. And, too, sitting in church beside Eric and pretending they were just friends would be impossible. Yet it wouldn't look right to sit elsewhere.

The following week, she threw herself into her work with an even greater fervor, knowing she benefited by the personal contact with people, needing their response to her as much as they needed her help. During the week, John handed her a key to a van, giving her permission to use it anytime it wasn't needed by the Center. She was grateful for that additional convenience.

Normally, she and Maila got together on Wednesday or Thursday, but the week slid by without any communication. Early Friday morning Maila called and asked Stacey to come to her apartment after work. A dread stirred in her heart at the serious tone in the girl's voice.

After work, without changing from the jeans and workshirt she had worn to the village, Stacey drove the van, stopped for hamburgers, then went to Maila's apartment.

She held her breath when the door opened, fearing Eric had felt a compulsion to "confess." Maila welcomed her as always, with warmth in her eyes.

While eating hamburgers, they joined in trivial

140

banter, then more serious matters as the discussion moved from work at the center, to the hospital, and their families. Maila had baked peanut butter cookies and made fresh coffee.

After a momentary silence, Stacey sensed something was not quite right.

"I need to talk to you, Stacey," Maila began hesitantly. "I don't really know how to begin."

Stacey lowered her eyes to the plate of cookies, half consumed.

"It's about Eric," Maila said, and Stacey felt herself go numb.

She forced herself to make eye contact with her friend. "What about him, Maila?"

"He took me out to dinner last night."

"And?"

Maila shrugged. "That's just it. That's all. He's never just called me up and taken me out to dinner. Alone. Without a reason."

"I don't understand, Maila," Stacey said. "What happened?"

"Oh, nothing happened, I mean, that's not the problem. Well, there's no problem, really. Except . . ."

"Just tell me, Maila. The best you can."

Maila's smile was weak, more a look of irony than pleasure. "I think it's started," she said.

"It?"

"You know I told you that my family, and Orlando, always said Eric was waiting for me to grow up before he made a move toward marriage. He must be making that move."

Stacey drew in her breath, wanting to ask what he said, what he did, and yet she didn't really want to know. But this should be no surprise. It's what she expected all along, and it was she who had helped Eric realize how much Maila really meant to him. He had even thanked her for it.

"He asked about my future plans," Maila was saying. "He wanted to know if I dreamed of becoming a doctor or wanted to go into another phase of medicine. I asked if he thought I should, and he said that was up to me. So I told him I'm happy where I am, as an RN." Her voice fell as she added, "Then he said he has applied for a transfer to America."

"Wouldn't you like that, Maila?"

Maila signed. "I always thought that would be the most marvelous thing in the world. To go to America. It's like a fantasyland." She began to pick at the peanut butter cookie on her plate. "That's what it was, Stacey. After my family began to tell me that Eric would someday marry me, I daydreamed about living at the villa, being a grand lady, having servants, like Francine was with you."

Stacey laughed suddenly. "That's not always ideal, Maila."

Maila smiled, as if remembering Stacey's total lack of privacy. "I realize that now, but those were the foolish dreams of a young girl. Like being famous or being a millionaire. It wasn't reality. This is."

Stacey watched as Maila's finger absently moved the crumbs around her plate. "You don't want to go to America now, Maila?"

She looked over at Stacey imploringly, and sighed. "I don't know if I could fit in. I have a place here in the Philippines, and a service to my people. Americans wouldn't need me."

"Oh, Maila, of course they do. America has needy people. They get sick."

She was shaking her head. "It's not the same."

"Did you tell Eric how you feel?"

"Oh, no," Maila said quickly, wide-eyed. "I wouldn't do that. We don't always speak the same language. There are things that can be said in Tagalog that cannot be said in English. But that's not what I mean by speaking the same language."

Stacey nodded her understanding.

"I don't always know what to say to him. With some people I can discuss my earlier life of poverty and laugh about certain aspects of it. I cannot laugh about poverty with Eric. He says something like, "We'll have to get that truck fixed so your father will never have to walk five miles in the rain again." Maila smiled. "With some people, we would laugh, even though it's serious."

Stacey knew instinctively that she would go to America, stay in the Philippines, or transfer to a remote part of the world without a question if Eric wanted her as his wife. But her heart went out to Maila, whose lifestyle and background were so unlike her own. And, Eric had implied she thought more like an Oriental than an American. Then she remembered a friend who had even been reluctant to leave her hometown and move to a nearby city. People were different, and she must try and concentrate on her friend's problems. "Are you afraid you don't have things in common with Eric?"

"I know I don't. I could see it even more clearly when you came, Stacey. You and he are so free and easy with each other. You laugh and joke and understand things that I'm not even sure about. I love watching you two. It's like an education. And I wonder if you're the kind of woman Eric should have, rather than me."

Stacey wished she were not in this position. Suppose she agreed. Would Maila step out of the picture? But she mustn't give into that temptation. She couldn't live with such a thing on her conscience.

"Opposites attract, so I've heard, Maila. And I can understand a man like Eric could want a woman like you. He is aware that most American women are very independent and refuse to be dominated. But you have such a gentle nature. I can understand that an

143

extrovert like him with all his activities and regimented lifestyle, would like to come home in the evening, not to be confronted by a cold stove and a career wife, but to someone who stays at home."

"With Eric, that's what I would be. But that's only a part of me, Stacey. With Filipinos, I'm more like you. A career woman and independent. To Eric, being a nurse is nothing spectacular, just a job with a worthwhile purpose. But some people, like Tomas, and. . . the workers at the villa . . . see me as," she blushed to say it, "Florence Nightengale."

Yes, it did seem that way at the villa, Stacey remembered. And it had been a part of Orlando's attitude. "Maila," she asked softly, "don't you want to marry Eric?"

"I don't know how to say this, Stacey," she began hesitantly. "I always thought I accepted that. It would be good for me, my family, and so many other people. But that would be here, not in America. And I never considered the ... married ... part. At least, not often. But when I did," she lowered her eyes and her voice, "it wasn't Eric."

"Orlando?"

"That's terrible, isn't it?"

Stacey reached over and covered her hand with her own. "We can't always control our thoughts, Maila. It's what we do about it that counts."

Maila nodded. Stacey got up to pour another cup of coffee for each of them. Pouring from the pot, she asked, "So you don't know which one you love most? Is that it, Maila?"

"It's not a matter of love, Stacey. It's a matter of what is best. Orlando doesn't love me now, so that is not even a consideration. And can you imagine, Stacey, if Eric asks me to marry him that I could say no?"

Stacey stared at her from over the cup then

carefully set it on the table. "No," she said honestly. "I cannot imagine that." She had just told Maila one couldn't always control one's thoughts, but at this moment she was trying desperately to be the kind of friend Maila needed. "My mom has said many times, Maila, that the kind of love two people feel when they marry is not the deep, abiding kind they have after living together for years, sharing experiences, getting to know and accept each other. I'm sure you and Eric would do everything in your power to have a good marriage and make your love grow."

Maila agreed. "I suppose I'm just scared."

"It's a big step," Stacey replied. "But, Maila, you deserve to be loved for yourself. You don't have to live up to a standard. You don't owe Eric, or anyone else, your life."

A determined look came into Maila's eyes. "Yes, I do, Stacey. The way we lived when I was young isn't life. It's existence, and not a very pleasant one. Yes, I do owe my life. To you, and to Eric." She inhaled, then spoke with a new confidence. "I guess I just needed to say it to someone. Of course, if Eric asks me to marry him, there's nothing to say but yes."

CHAPTER 9

MAILA DID NOT CALL during the week, and Stacey could only surmise she was seeing Eric on her days off. The end of the week brought a surprise.

John said, "Eric has invited several of the children to go to the base on Saturday and see the ships." Stacey didn't understand his discomfort until he added, "He said that Maila will join us. She managed to exchange shifts with another nurse."

Stacey turned from him quickly as if to look through some letters on the desk in front of her. She looked straight into the face of Maureen, and realized that was probably worse. The woman was very perceptive. Stacey spoke quickly. "I had planned to take Fredrico to a matinee, but I know he'd rather see the ships."

"You can go with us, Stacey," Maureen said, watching her curiously.

She shook her head. "I'd rather not."

"It's a morning outing, Stacey," John said, walking over to the desk. "Someone can drop him off at your

146

apartment and you can still make the movie, if you'd like."

"That would be fine," she agreed. "Then I can drive him home later in the van."

"By the way," John said, "I haven't heard much from Eric lately. He hasn't been in church for the past two Sundays. Any idea what he's up to?"

"No. Yes." Stacey inhaled deeply. "I think he's seeing a lot of Maila."

"Maila?"

Stacey nodded and looked at Maureen, who asked, "Seeing? You mean seriously?"

"Yes," Stacey said. "That's how it appears."

'I never considered such a thing," John said. "I thought . . . I mean . . . well . . ."

"John," Maureen said quietly. He cleared his throat and pretended to look at the letters Stacey was moving from one stack to another, having no idea what was in them.

"Why not?" Stacey asked suddenly, in the awkward silence.

"No reason at all," Maureen said. "She's a fine young woman. Very dear to us all."

"Yes," John agreed.

On Saturday afternoon, when the van pulled up in front of her apartment and the horn blew, Stacey rushed outside, delighted to see Fredrico again. He jumped out and hugged her fervently around the waist. The smile left her face when Stacey stared ahead, surprised to see Orlando at the wheel of Farrington Farms van and Maila sitting in front.

"We had a wonderful tour. The children loved it!" Maila said brightly, but she looked very uncomfortable as her eyes met Stacey's.

Orlando simply stared straight ahead, until he started to drive away. His eyes cut around toward Stacey and their gaze held for a moment. There didn't seem to be any anger there, or bitterness, or warning. Only some kind of concern.

There was no time to think of anything then, but Fredrico. He was neither still nor quiet for a moment. He began to tell about the base and the ships. Stacey began to feel she had been on the tour herself.

A short while later they left the apartment to go into town. "Do you know that I love you?" she asked, as they stepped out into the bright afternoon sun.

He stared up at her for a minute, his dark eyes growing moist. Then he nodded, tucking his lips inward in a strange kind of grin and sighed heavily. "Me, too," he said low, then looked everywhere but at her.

She tousled his curls. "Let's go to a movie."

He ran for the van.

It was after she had taken a very happy little boy home and returned to the apartment that Maila called. Stacey almost hoped that Eric had proposed, Maila had accepted, and that it would be settled. But Orlando was the topic of conversation.

"I didn't think much about his picking me and Fredrico up this morning and taking us to the base. He often drives for Eric when he's in town. But, returning for us seemed . . . strange."

"Eric probably had business, Maila. Doesn't Orlando bring the books in when Eric doesn't go to the villa?"

"I think so. It's not that, really, Stacey. It's Orlando. He was so strange."

"You mean sullen and distant, as usual?"

There was a pause. "He was until after he dropped Fredrico off at your place. I was shocked when he started talking to me. He said Eric wants to make him manager of the farm, and will even make it possible for him to buy it if he wants to."

Stacey remembered Eric's idle comment that he might sell. "What did Orlando say?"

"That's what's so strange. I asked him and he answered with a question. He asked me if Eric had proposed, and I said no. He asked if we were dating and I said, well yes, I supposed so."

Stacey heard Maila's intake of breath before she continued. "Then he turned toward me, looked me right in the face and said that what he wanted more than anything in the world was my happiness."

"Then what, Maila?" Stacey encouraged, hearing her sniff.

"I told him I was happy. We just looked at each other, Stacey. I felt like it was seven years ago and the most incredible thing happened. I started to cry. It just couldn't stop and I didn't even wipe the tears away. Orlando stopped looking at me and I got out and ran into the apartment building where he couldn't see me. I have never behaved like this before," she wailed, bewildered. "I don't know what's happening to me."

Stacey knew she could not tell Maila how it looked to her. It wouldn't make any difference anyway. As long as there was a chance that Eric wanted to marry her, Maila would agree to it, no matter how she felt, no matter how Orlando felt. Maila was too close to see it all clearly. And Stacey felt she was in no position to counsel or advise anyone. Love, she realized, could be a very painful experience. And confusing.

Although hoping for the best, Stacey felt things grew increasingly worse during the following week. It began on Sunday morning when she had to go to the hut and be confronted by a still-drunk Nico who didn't know the whereabouts of his wife and son.

"You look so pale, Stacey. Are you all right?" Maureen asked when she returned to the car.

"My head has started to pound and I feel nauseous," she said, feeling her control about to break.

Maureen said they would return to the apartment.

John tried to console her, "Stacey, surely you couldn't expect Nico to change overnight. Not in his own strength. This was bound to happen. But he made an effort. You must see that as hope. He can try again. We mustn't expect too much, too soon."

"I know," she agreed, but it didn't make her feel any better at the moment.

Maureen went inside with Stacey and watched while she took something for the headache. "We're your friends, Stacey. You know you can talk to me, don't you?" she asked, and Stacey knew she was referring to things other than Nico.

"Yes," Stacey said gratefully. "I may need to do that."

"Anytime," Maureen said kindly.

But Stacey did not feel this was the time. She insisted Maureen go on to church.

She didn't know if it would be right to confide in Maureen about this. Both Eric and Maila were friends of the Carlsons. It was she who was the intruder. She who had known Maila loved Eric from the very first. She who should have kept her feelings under control from the beginning.

But no, she said to herself then. She had been defenseless against the feelings that had surfaced and grown since the moment she met Eric. She never intended to fall in love with him.

Then she felt as helpless as Maila had described over the phone. The tears started and she seemed to be crying about all the people and all the troubles of the world, and felt she would never stop.

John and Maureen's sympathetic kindness during the week did nothing to alleviate her misery. She had come to the Philippines to help other people, to be of service to them, and to earn her master's degree in Social Work. Now she felt it would have been better if she had stayed in America.

The Carlsons said she had taken on more responsibility than any of their other workers. She could only hope and pray her presence was of value. She sensed it was when Fredrico called to say he and his mother had returned home and his daddy wanted Stacey and the Carlsons to know that he was sorry the boy didn't get to go to church on Sunday.

Then, the heavens started to cry. It rained all day Thursday, Friday, and by Saturday there were severe storm warnings. The Weather Bureau reported a typhoon blowing up out of the Pacific toward the east and southeast. There were indications it might come inland as far as Manila.

By Saturday evening the three-story CF office building was packed with children and elderly people needing shelter from the rains and wind. All the talk was about the bagyos and past typhoons that had caused considerable damage through the islands. Stacey's mind was completely occupied with the care of the people whose families were out boarding up windows, sandbagging, and getting others to the safety of sturdy buildings and church basements.

As the busses and vans came, and went, she checked lists to insure that all the sponsored families were accounted for. Maureen assured Stacey that Maila would be at the hospital for the duration of the storm.

The worst was expected to hit during the night, and already reports had come in that a fishing village along the coast had been completely wiped out, and the loss of life was extensive. The torrential rains flooded rice fields, washed roads away, and left others impassable.

The swirling mass of wind and water was slowly making its way over the land. An edge of it would certainly hit Manila, with the greater force to the north.

"That's where the base is," Stacey said with

concern when she had a chance to stop for a cup of coffee and speak to Maureen.

"Yes, but it's probably the safest place to be. Don't worry about Eric. He called earlier and I assured him we would take good care of you."

Stacey looked away from the warmth in Maureen's eyes, and down at her coffee. "That's nice of him." Then she smiled over at Maureen, adding, "and of you."

"Mmmm," Maureen said skeptically, rolling her eyes toward the sound of wind rattling the windows. "I just hope I can keep that promise."

Orlando, Tomas, and some of the other farm workers, who were familiar with the area had come early Saturday morning to drive vans into remote sections, transporting people to safety. Stacey recalled that such a storm as this had caused the flood damage leading to the destruction of Mr. Molino's farms.

Later in the evening, when the gray of dusk had deepened to night, Orlando stood before Stacey, while she made a final check of names. "Fredrico isn't here," she noted, turning the paper to read a note scribbled in the margin. *Father wouldn't cooperate.* She looked at Orlando, her eyes fearful. "I can't let that child stay in that little hut during this storm."

"I'll go," Orlando volunteered.

She shook her head. "You've been out all day. This is personal to me. I have to do it."

"You couldn't even find your way through the flooded streets of Manila," he said roughly.

"It's really too dangerous for anyone to go out again, Orlando," she said with exasperated resignation. "We'll just have to wait, and pray."

He shook his head. "It doesn't matter to me. It's worth the chance. I have no real future."

"But, Orlando," she said cautiously, never quite

sure what to say to him, "hasn't Eric offered to make you manager, or even sell part of the farm to you?"

"I can't stay now," he said, "now that it's begun to happen. They're seeing each other. I don't want to watch it."

"But that's what you wanted," Stacey protested.

"It's not what I want in my heart. I try to do what is best for her. It's hard to give up someone you love. Is it not?"

She saw the pain in his eyes, the resignation, the nobility. "I'll go with you," she said.

"No," he said. "You do a good work with people. Your life matters. Mine does not."

She started to refute that, but knew her words would mean nothing to Orlando. He was stubborn and wanted to do this noble thing.

Reaching out, she grasped his wet shoulders and hugged him.

He looked surprised, then turned red, "You would be my second choice for Commander Farrington," he said, then left the room.

That was quite a compliment, coming from Orlando. Stacey appreciated it. But she could not allow herself to be second with Eric. Her own fragile heart could not bear the pain.

The long night passed slowly. The lights and phones went out. Several windows on the third level broke from the force of the wind and had to be covered with canvas. Water oozed around the edges and made puddles on the floor.

Most of the children slept soundly on mats. Adults were quiet, but restless. The building wheezed and groaned in protest to the force of the eerie howling wind. Several times Stacey looked out but saw nothing except water splashing against the window-panes.

Lying on a mat, she dozed occasionally, but awoke

153

each time with a start, wondering if she heard the sound of a van. But Orlando did not return.

Exhaustion settled in the form of slumber on the weary occupants as the wind finally expended its energy and slowly retreated from the city, heading out toward the South China Sea. By morning, the sky turned a light gray, and steady rain fell onto the streams of water rushing around buildings, collecting debris and hiding the streets.

"Orlando probably took Fredrico and his family to the nearest shelter, Stacey," Maureen said reassuringly, but her tired eyes looked as doubtful as Stacey felt. Tomas went out to look, saying he also needed to check with Maila and find a phone so he could call his family.

Time passed swiftly with their having to feed the many people without the aid of electricity for cooking. As soon as breakfast was finished, preparations for a cold lunch began. By afternoon power was restored, but not the phones. Tomas returned around three o'clock.

"You found them?" Stacey asked urgently, impatient with Tomas' hesitance.

"Yes, and the boy's going to be fine," he said, but his eyes and expression indicated that things were not so fine.

"Going to be?" she asked, concerned.

"There was an accident, but he will be all right."

"Is Orlando all right? What about Maria and Nico?"

Tomas shrugged helplessly and would not meet her eyes. "Commander Farrington said he would tell you when you get to the hospital."

"Hospital?" she almost shrieked, her heart pounding. "Is he hurt?"

"No," he said quickly, "but Maila called him. She's very upset."

154

"Upset?"

He nodded. "Orlando is hurt. Bad."

Maureen, who had been listening, insisted Stacey go to the hospital with Tomas. "Fredrico has become so attached to you, Stacey. He may need you. We'll handle things here."

Brilliant sunshine and the fresh cool breeze belied the tragic toll the storm had taken the night before. White clouds dotted the blue sky. Everything appeared clean and shining. The landscape, however, bore the evidence with an occasional uprooted tree, many broken limbs, repairmen perched high on poles, puddles in the middle of an otherwise dry street and water standing along the sides of roads and buildings. Weary people trudged the streets in dirty, wrinkled work clothes, rather than their usual Sunday finery.

At the hospital Tomas approached the nurse's station and asked that Eric be paged. "He's been talking with the doctors all morning, finding out what he can about Orlando and Fredrico," he told her, then led her to a waiting room where several people whispered quietly. He left after saying he needed to check on Maila and find out if Mrs. Molino had arrived.

Stacey stood at a window, staring outside, trying not to worry, when she heard his voice.

"Stacey," he said quietly.

She turned as Eric, in a blue uniform, stood beside her.

"Fredrico," she whispered anxiously. "What happened to him?"

"He will recover." But she saw the concern in his eyes. He inhaled deeply before continuing. "When the rescue squad found the van this morning, it was wedged in a clump of trees. Not too far from where Fredrico lived. Nico. . ." He stopped. "Come sit down."

They sat on a nearby couch. Her questioning eyes urged him to continue. She wished he had not. "There was a fire in the house. Nico id dead." he said.

Stacey gasped, astonished.

His tired eyes gazed into hers and his voice was weary. "We can only try and piece things together, but it must have happened before Orlando got there."

"And Fredrico?"

"His feet are blistered. The extent of the damage is uncertain at the moment, but the doctors assured me there will be no permanent damage. And he has a broken leg. We surmise his many bruises occurred as a result of being thrown around in the van."

"Maria?"

The lines at the corners of Eric's eyes deepened. He sighed heavily. "She died a short while ago."

A wave of anguish swept over Stacey. Closing her eyes, she asked, "Does he know?"

Eric replied, "We thought it best to wait."

Wait? For what? How long? Then her startled eyes opened and met his. "For . . . for me?"

He nodded.

Fearful of giving way to the fatigue threatening to overtake her, Stacey covered her face with her hands for a moment, then clasped them tightly on her lap. "I don't think I'm the one," she admitted to herself as much as to Eric. "So many situations here have required more than I feel capable of giving." Her voice dropped to a whisper. "I don't feel adequate."

"We're all about pushed to the limit, Stacey," he consoled. "You need rest. Perhaps you'll feel differently after you've had some sleep." Sighing, he looked around. "There should be a coffee machine around here somewhere. I'll be right back."

Her eyes focused on the wrinkled shirt and dirty jeans she had worn all night and for two days. She realized suddenly how awful she must look, devoid of makeup and her hair twisted into a pony tail, secured with a rubber band.

"I guess you've seen me at my worst," she said, slightly embarrassed, after thanking him for the coffee he set on the table in front of the couch.

"No," he countered immediately, walking around to sit near her again. "You're more beautiful right now then you've ever been. When you see a person forgetting themselves, caring about other people, then you know their beauty is real."

She knew he was talking about the cooperation and teamwork of so many during the past days. Especially those like Orlando, who could have remained in a place of safety. Stacey met Eric's steady gaze and replied seriously, "I've seen a lot of beautiful people lately."

Eric smiled in agreement. "The human race is often amazingly beneficent."

Stacey reached for her coffee, sipped it, and realized her hands weren't altogether steady. She had forced herself to eat part of a sandwich at lunchtime, but she couldn't stop to eat while there were so many pressing matters at hand. The creamy coffee helped to fill the empty spot in her stomach.

She set the cup down and stared at it. "You must have been awake all night too, Eric. You don't need to stay with me. I know you have many people to be concerned about."

"Yes," he interrupted immediately, setting his cup down. "And you're one of them. The first person, in fact, that I thought about when the storm became threatening." Reaching over, he took her trembling hand in his. "You've woven your way into our lives and our hearts, Stacey. How could I not be concerned?"

Stacey closed her eyes against the soothing effect of his beautiful words. His "our" meant not just himself, but also Maila, the Carlsons, perhaps the people she worked with through the CF office, and especially Fredrico. It had been she who had placed too much personal significance on his acceptance and caring. Her own emotions had become so tangled she wasn't sure how to deal with them. But despite her feelings, she must try and live up to the faith so many had placed in her.

She inhaled deeply. "Eric, perhaps I am the one to tell Fredrico. And he has a right to know as soon as possible."

Eric agreed and stood, taking away the warmth of his hand from hers. "Let's stop by the nurse's station, then I'll show you his ward. I need to check on some other matters and will meet you here in the waiting room later."

Stacey saw Fredrico before he saw her. She walked between rows of bedfast children, down to the sixth bed on the right. He lay flat, his head on a pillow, his eyes closed. The broken leg was elevated in a metal contraption and the other was stretched out. Both feet were terribly blistered and swollen. The right one was worse, with red, raw places. The heel lay on a gauze bandage.

This was only the physical, she reminded herself. How much more pain this little boy would feel in his heart when he learned he had lost both parents.

"Pretty ugly, huh?" his voice piped up and Stacey looked up to see big black eyes watching her.

Taking a deep breath, she forced a smile and walked to the side of the bed. "But I understand they will heal all right."

"Yea," he agreed. "They think so. But it will take awhile and it will hurt too. They couldn't put a regular cast on my leg, so I'll have to be careful about that."

"Does it hurt a lot?" she asked, reaching over for the chair at a small table by the wall. She turned it to face the bed and sat down.

"Not too much," he said bravely. "But it's supposed to." His eyes grew bigger. "It's okay if my leg doesn't hurt. But this one," he pointed to the right foot, "If it hurts, it's a good sign that I have the right kind of feeling in it and will walk all right later on."

His amount of information surprised her. "The doctors must have told you a lot."

"They didn't at first, when I asked. But after Commander Farrington came, he told me he was getting the best doctors there are, whatever it takes to make me well again. I told him I needed to know how bad my feet are. They don't look too good." He wrinkled his nose, looking toward them.

"I told him I needed to know, because it would be foolish to pray about blisters, if I needed to pray about walking again."

"That makes sense," Stacey said quickly, looking down at the bed, resisting the urge to take him in her arms and cry like a baby.

"Commander Farrington said he would talk to the doctor. It wasn't long before the doctor came back. He pulled up that chair you're sitting in and talked to me a long time about it. Before he left he asked me to pray for him, too, and I said I sure would."

Whatever words she was about to say were stopped when he added, "My daddy's dead."

She didn't know how to respond, and he asked, "Did you know that?"

"Yes, but I don't know what happened."

Fredrico shifted his gaze toward the wall. "Pull the curtains, and I'll tell you. I don't think these little kids need to hear this."

Stacey pulled the curtains around both sides of his bed and returned to the chair. How incredible that she felt like the patient and Fredrico, the comforter.

He told her the story, most of the time looking at a spot on the curtain beyond his feet. But Stacey knew that's not what he was seeing.

Nico wouldn't let them go with the CF bus drivers, saying he had been through storms before and would take care of his own family. He would not go to a church basement in the village. The trees would shelter them from wind and rain. The storm would pass.

As it grew worse toward evening, Maria begged to take Fredrico to the village. Nico said go. But the wind was too strong and the rain so heavy they couldn't see. Nico began to drink. For a while Fredrico and his mother huddled in a dry corner, and he played the ukelele and sang to her. Then Nico made him stop.

The wind blew the covering from the window, and seemed to lift the house off the piles, but it settled again. Before Maria could reach the lantern to extinguish the light, it sailed across the room to where Nico lay on the mat. The oil spilled out and flames immediately engulfed the entire corner.

Maria screamed and tried to awaken Nico, to no avail. Rain began to pour in while the wind whipped the flames around the room.

Fredrico wasn't sure if they ran out the door opening, or window, or if the floor caved in. But the next thing he knew, he and Maria had crawled away from the charred mass of smouldering wet thatch. What was left began to be blown or washed away. The rain put out the flames on their clothes.

Fredrico lay on the ground, hanging onto a tree trunk. Maria lay beside him.

"I didn't know my feet were burned," Fredrico said now. "It seemed a long time later when I saw lights shining through the trees. Orlando took Mama first, then came back for me. I sat on the floor in the back and talked to Mama. She just moaned. Then the van started to roll over and over. I didn't think Mama knew what was going on, but she got her arms around

160

me and wouldn't let go. I guess that's why I don't have more than a broken leg. You think so?"

"Yes," Stacey whispered hoarsely. "I think so."

He gulped hard. "Is Orlando okay?"

She told him what the doctors said about Orlando and knew what his next question would be.

"Is my mama dead?"

Stacey nodded. "Her burns were bad, but it was mainly internal injuries. She probably got those when the van rolled over."

His face contorted into a grimace. "When she was saving my life," he said, looking down at his hands that gripped the bed cover so hard his knuckles were white.

"It's all right to cry, Fredrico," Stacey said quietly. She reached over for his tight little fist.

"Yeah," he agreed, swallowing hard, "I guess I will, later, I think I need to, but right now it kinda hurts too much. Right in here." His hand came up to his chest and throat. "In a way it's like a movie. Not really real."

Stacey held his hand tightly. He put his other on top of hers. "My ukelele's gone," he said unevenly. Then the tears spilled over onto his cheeks. His little lips trembled. His breath was ragged as he gasped for air.

"Fredrico, my darling boy," she breathed, reaching over to hold him. His arms came around her neck and his cheek lay next to hers as he sobbed brokenly. Her heart went out to the little boy swallowed up in a grayish, wrinkled hospital gown. She could do something about that, but it would be impossible to prevent the pain Fredrico must yet endure. She could only share in it.

Later, after a nurse came in to give him his medication, he grew drowsy. "I'll see you in the morning," she told him, and kissed him on the cheek.

When she returned to the waiting room, Eric and

Mrs. Molino were sitting on a couch. Tomas stood nearby, his hands clasped in front of him. Hearing a sound, Stacey turned toward the doorway. Maila, eyes red and swollen, rushed inside.

Although dressed in her white uniform, the demeanor of a professional nurse had completely disappeared. Distress clearly outlined her face. "It's what the doctors feared," she gasped. "Orlando is still in a coma and he . . . he has . . . pneumonia. He's . . ." her breath wouldn't seem to come. "He's . . ." By that time Tomas's quick strides brought him to her side. Stacey reached out toward her. Eric turned toward Mrs. Molino, who's great sob seemed to shake the room, and Maila lost all consciousness.

CHAPTER 10

As soon as Tomas dropped her off at the apartment, Stacey called her parents. They were glad to hear her voice, but John Carlson had talked with them earlier.

"He said you were fine, invaluable to them, and tired," her father said. Stacey detected the pride in his voice.

"Randy has been in touch," her mother said hesitantly. "Is there anything in particular you'd like us to tell him?"

"No, mother. There isn't. And I'll call you tomorrow with details."

"Now you get your rest," her father ordered.

"Yes, Dad," she said congenially. "I love you both."

"We love you," they said in unison.

Stacey smiled at the phone after hanging up. It was wonderful hearing their voices. It seemed a million years ago since she had left that secure, relatively peaceful existence in Carbondale, Illinois. Her involvement with foreign students was, at times, very demanding. But her greatest worry had been over Randy. Now that, too, seemed minor compared with the pressing concerns that existed here.

She called the Carlsons' home and a grateful sigh escaped her lips to discover they were not still at the CF office. "Everything's under control," Maureen said. "John and I are going in late in the morning and you have the day off."

That would work well with Stacey's plans. "I do want to stop by and talk with you about Fredrico, if you have the time."

"Of course," Maureen replied. "I didn't think you'd spend the day on yourself." Then her voice grew more serious. "We've heard about Fredrico. And Eric said you were telling him about his parents."

Stacey told her what had transpired. And about Orlando.

"We'll be praying," Maureen assured her.

"Oh, yes, tell John I appreciate his calling my parents. I didn't think of it until tonight."

"He thought you would have other things on your mind, Stacey. Now, try to sleep tonight."

"I don't think I could help it," she laughed, though wearily.

After a soothing warm bath and a supper of orange juice, milk, scrambled eggs, and toast, Stacey lounged on her couch in her terry robe, listening to the TV accounts of the storm. Despite the many tragedies around Manila, she realized they were few compared with the damage done to lives and property along the coast.

She had just finished a cup of coffee when the phone rang and she jumped. That phone had more activity in this one night than in the entire time she had been in the Philippines.

"Hello?"

"Stacey." Eric's deep voice was a balm. "Hope you weren't asleep."

"No. I'll have to rest awhile before I can sleep."

He chuckled slightly. "I know the feeling."

Then she gripped the receiver tightly. "Is something wrong?" she asked suddenly.

"No, it's just that the base will not be on regular schedule tomorrow, and I wondered if you thought Fredrico might like a present."

"I'm sure he would, Eric. I thought I would try to find a ukelele for him."

"What if I pick you up in the morning and we shop together? You would be a big help to me."

"Know anything about ukelele's?" she asked.

He laughed. "I know how to find out. About nine o'clock?"

She said that would be fine and said good night.

Her mind wouldn't stay on the TV program, nor on the journal she got and held on her lap. She thought of Maila, and how embarrassed she had been to discover she collapsed right there in front of everyone.

Stacy called Maila. "I just wanted to check on you, Maila."

"Mrs. Molino and I are eating supper, Stacey. It's good having her stay with me. We really will get a good night's sleep. They gave me tomorrow off since I worked over the weekend."

"I'll be praying about*everything*, Maila," Stacey told her.

"Thanks," she said gratefully. "We're doing that, too."

Stacey fell asleep saying her prayers and awoke the next morning with a heavy head and stiff muscles. After stretching exercises, a shower and coffee, she felt like coping with whatever the day might bring.

Wanting a light and unencumbered feeling, she chose a yellow sundress with gray embroidered flowers bordering the v-yoke. The gathered skirt had side pockets and a deep flounce falling to below her knees. She slipped into pumps and added bangle bracelets and white earrings. It felt good to be out of jeans for a change.

She opened the door to Eric's knock, and stepped into the cool, sunny morning.

"Marked change from yesterday," he said approvingly, scanning her appearance.

Stacey stopped at the car door. "My mother taught me that if something goes wrong in one area, don't droop. She says do something constructive for yourself." She lifted her face toward the sky and looked at the fluffy white clouds. "This is the kind of day that she would buy a new dress or get a new hairdo."

Eric grimaced. "I won't have to wait for that, will I?"

Her laughing brown eyes met his. "Not today. There isn't time." She slid into the seat and he closed the door after her.

Their easy comraderie, and the twinkling acceptance in his eyes reminded her of the day he took her sightseeing. But it couldn't end the same, and she mustn't think like that.

Eric drove to a shop that sold musical instruments and talked for a long time to the proprietor about ukeleles. Stacey explained the boy's ear for music and ability to pick out melodies from complicated tunes.

They chose a ukelele. While the proprietor put it in a bag, Eric turned to Stacey. "Perhaps we could have an instructor go to the hospital an hour or so several times a week to give Fredrico lessons."

A sound of pleasure escaped Stacey's throat. "Eric, what a wonderful idea!"

He shrugged it off. "When he's adept at that, we can go on to other musical instruments."

"Will that be all, sir?" the proprietor asked.

Eric's cheeks dimpled as he continued to look at Stacey. "For now," he said.

Stacey looked over and touched an instrument she knew nothing about, pretending to be interested.

"Now what?" he asked, when they were outside on the sidewalk.

"Ships!" she said, holding her hands out as if to ask, "what else?"

Eric laughed. "Those are in the car. Destroyers, aircraft carriers, cruisers, submarines, to name a few. All he has to do is build them."

Stacey smiled her approval. "Oh, I know," she said then. "Books. Let's find a bookstore."

A short while later, laden with packages, they returned to the car. When they neared the hospital, Stacey felt the weight of the burden again.

After coming to a stop in the parking lot, Eric turned toward her on the seat. "Why that dejected look, Stacey?" he asked quietly.

"I didn't mean for it to show," she confessed. "I was thinking about how Fredrico will be the most entertaining little fellow around with his ukelele." A softness touched her face and she smiled wryly. "He already is," she addded. "But as he grows older, he will learn technique. That will mean so much."

She inhaled deeply and blinked away the moisture that threatened to gather in her eyes. "Then I thought about where he would be. In an orphanage? With foster parents who don't really understand his background? Oh, Eric."

"Stacey," he said quietly. "Don't you known that the Carlsons and I will make certain that boy is taken care of properly?"

She closed her eyes against his reprimand, and his intense blue eyes that reached her heart. "Yes," she whispered. "It's just that I won't be here to know."

"How long?"

"Three weeks, after this one," she said and bit on her lip.

"Three weeks," he said distantly, looking beyond her. "Then you can return to a normal way of life, without all the demands that have been imposed upon you here."

She shook her head. "I don't want that normal way of life anymore."

His eyes returned to her so quickly, she thought perhaps he misunderstood her. "Oh, Eric, of course I don't welcome such tragedies. What I mean is, I want to be involved where I'm really needed."

"I know what you mean," he replied immediately. "And you're needed here. Don't doubt that for a minute. Now," he said, smiling suddenly, "we'd better get these packages inside." He turned and reached for the door handle.

Stacey hugged Fredrico, and Eric shook his hand.

"This is great," Fredrico exclaimed, excited, looking at the picture of the aircraft carrier, complete with its own planes. "Look, Carlo." He held it out for a boy two beds away to see, then turned back to Eric. "He likes ships and planes. You wanna show him this?"

'Sure," Eric said, smiling and took the box down to Carlo.

"Super," Carlo said, big-eyed. "Can I watch you put it together?"

"You can help me," Fredrico promised. He looked at the books. They were Bible stories, mainly in pictures. "Can everybody see?" he asked.

Stacey nodded. "I thought you'd want that. Shall I pass them out?"

"'All of them," Fredrico said.

Eric handed him the ukelele and Fredrico stared at it on his lap. His hand touched the strings, but made no sound. Stacey and Eric exchanged confused glances, uncertain whether or not he liked it. Perhaps not. The old one had sentimental value. It couldn't really be replaced. Just as presents couldn't replace his parents.

"Here. I can put it by the table, Fredrico."

He handed her the ukelele.

"It's not that I don't like it," he said, looking from Stacey to Eric. "It's what I want more than anything. I mean," he corrected, "more than anything you could buy for me. But I think I should wait."

"Wait?" Eric asked kindly.

Fredrico drew a deep breath, his eyes imploring Eric to understand. "The preacher and the doctor said they would talk to you about a . . ." he hesitated, as if trying to think of the word, "about a service tomorrow. I want to wait until after that before I play it. Because, you see, the last thing my daddy said to me was not to play the ukelele." His black eyes darted from one to the other. "He didn't mean never play it. Just that night. He really liked it sometimes."

"Son," Eric said quietly, moving closer to touch Fredrico's shoulder, "that's a very respectful thing for you to do. Your father, and your mother, would be proud of you."

"You think they know?" he asked with trembly lips.

"Yes," Eric said with conviction. "I would say they do. Now, would you like to talk about the service?"

Fredrico nodded. Eric pulled up the chair, sat down, and made his suggestions.

Stacey inhaled deeply, blinked back the tears and turned to the little boy in the bed next to Fredrico's. She began to talk to him about the picture book he so eagerly devoured with his eyes.

"Eric, you handled that so beautifully," Stacey said after they left the ward. "I would have taken him in my arms like I did last night and cried with him. You treated him like a little man."

'He's both, Stacey," Eric assured her. "And he needs both. I suppose we all do. We don't seem to grow too old to cry."

"You're right," Stacey agreed. "I've cried more in the past week or so than in my entire life."

She glanced at him quickly, and held her breath, lest he ask the reason for her tears. Fredrico's tragedy happened only yesterday. But he looked straight ahead, a thoughtful expression on his face.

"Have you heard any more about Orlando's condition?" she asked.

He shook his head. "I need to check while we're here."

After Eric talked with a doctor he returned to say there was no change. "There's nothing new they could tell me. Orlando hasn't regained consciousness." He appeared worried. 'The pneumonia is a complicating factor."

On Tuesday, the brief memorial service was held in the small chapel. Maureen and John, along with the CF office workers, came. So did the pastor and his wife from the village near where Fredrico had lived. Mrs. Molino and Maila sat near the back. With special permission, Carlo attended. Fredrico sat in a wheel chair at the front, between Eric and Stacey.

Several wreaths of flowers had been placed around the podium from where the preacher said a few words about death being an inevitable part of life, and how one needs Jesus as his personal Saviour in order to live the abundant life. He spoke of God's love, forgiveness, and eternity. It was a message of encouragement to the living.

By the end of the week, Fredrico's feet looked worse. His blisters were turning to sores and beginning to scab. That was part of the healing process.

The ukelele became a vital part of the children's activities. They sang the songs Fredrico taught them, while he played.

The greatest concern of the moment was Orlando. While Stacey visited with Fredrico on Friday night, Maureen and John came in, saying they would stay for awhile. Maila wanted her to come to the waiting room on the floor where Orlando's room was located.

Upon entering, she was confronted with three silent people on the couch. Maila sat between Eric and Mrs. Molino. Tomas, in his farm workclothes, leaned against a wall. Each looked at her as she approached and she saw the concern in Eric's eyes, the distress in Maila's, the quiet grief in Mrs. Molino's. Tomas' gaze returned to the floor beyond his shoes.

Eric stood, motioning for her to sit beside Maila. "How is he?" Stacey asked, taking the seat.

Maila twisted the handkerchief in her hands. "The doctor just talked to us. He's in and out of the coma now." She gulped miserably, her words came haltingly. "They say . . . he's . . . lost the will to live. He's not fighting. Not . . . trying." Fresh tears poured from her eyes.

Mrs. Molino reached over and grasped Maila's hand. "You can help my boy." Her quiet affirmation stunned them all for a moment.

Maila's swollen eyes slowly turned to Mrs. Molino, who simply stared at a spot on the floor. "I . . . can't," she whispered.

Then in the thick silence, Tomas said quietly. "Maila, you're the only one who can."

Maila gasped and stared at her brother, grieving for his friend. "Tomas," she pleaded, moving her head helplessly. Then she turned to Stacey. "What can I do?"

Stacey closed her eyes against the temptation to tell Maila they were right about her being able to give

171

Orlando a reason to live. But how much of her advice would be selfish motive? What did Eric really want? What was best? And right? "I'm not the one to say, Maila. I'm sorry."

Eric came over and knelt in front of Maila. Stacey got up and walked over to the window distancing herself from the touching tableau.

Taking Maila's hand in his, Eric said, "Listen to me, Maila. I can't make your decisions for you. But I will try to advise you as I feel a . . . a father would do."

Stacey saw the sudden lift of Maila's gaze from her hand to Eric's eyes when he said "father," and an element of confusion blended with her emotional turmoil.

"Orlando is dying," he said quietly, "and he's too young, with much to live for. But now, he's at a disadvantage because of his weakened physical condition. He's not competent to make life and death decisions. If you can help him, Maila, then you must do so. Whatever conflict there may be, can be dealt with later on."

The moisture dried on her face as she stared at Eric. "I'll try," she whispered faintly.

Standing, he held out his hand to help her up. Tomas came over and put his arm around her shoulders and they walked from the room together.

Stacey knew that if Orlando died, Maila would need Eric even more. Feeling like an intruder, she walked out into the hallway. Tomas stood outside a door.

When Maila came out, Stacey hurried to reach her. Maila fell into her brother's arms and sobbed against his chest. Stacey placed a comforting hand on her arm.

Finally, lifting her head, she looked from Tomas to Stacey. "I talked to him," she said, the anguish etched on her face and in her voice. "But I don't think he even heard me."

After Maureen and John dropped her off at the apartment, Stacey called her parents. She promised to write the details, but she had decided she wanted to adopt Fredrico and care for him in the States.

Her father reminded her of the ramifications, encouraged her to get away from the situation and think about it with a clear head. But he concluded in the way she had expected. "Since you're single, Stacey," he said. "it would be simpler for your mother and me to adopt the boy. And you know, we will help any way possible."

"This may seem trivial now, Stacey, but it's very important," her mother added. "You need to remember the man you may someday marry will have to be the kind who wouldn't mind taking on a ready-made family."

"Yes, mother, I know," Stacey replied with a determined confidence in her voice. "I wouldn't want any other kind of man."

On Monday, when Stacey related her plans to Maureen and John, they were enthusiastic, saying they would check into the possibilities. But late that evening when Maureen called, her attitude was entirely different.

"Perhaps John and I spoke too soon, Stacey. You see, I had to consult with Eric about the possibility of adoption. Fredrico's sponsorship was transferred to him, and he's taking care of medical expenses. We have to consider his opinion."

Such a development had not occurred to Stacey. "He . . . he doesn't approve?"

Maureen hesitated, before saying, "It's very unclear to me, Stacey. Eric was surprised. Then thoughtful. Perhaps I approached him at the wrong time."

"Wrong time?" Stacey questioned, unable to fathom that a certain time or approach would be necessary.

Maureen tried to explain. "He has so much on his mind, Stacey. The farm. Orlando. Fredrico . . ."

"Then he thought the adoption was not a good idea?" Stacey asked, her spirits drooping.

"He said something about having to discuss it with you and mumbled something about it being a big job for a single parent."

"But Maureen," Stacey objected. "One parent is better than . . . than none."

Maureen's concern was reflected in her voice. "He probably didn't even know what I said, Stacey."

But he did know, for a short while later Eric called. "I need to talk to you about Fredrico, Stacey. Could you meet me at the hospital tomorrow evening?"

"Yes, of course," she replied. 'Are . . .are you all right?"

"Orlando has regained consciousness a couple of times," he said, his voice elated. "I want to talk with him as soon as it's allowed."

"That's wonderful, Eric," she said. "I'm so glad."

"The doctors warned we mustn't get our hopes too high yet," he cautioned. "But it is improvement, Stacey."

The following evening Stacey took special care with her makeup, hoping to conceal whatever disappointment would inevitably show when Eric would tell her he didn't approve of her adopting Fredrico. She even curled her hair and was pleased with how the light brought out the gold in its tawny color. Like the make-up artist in Illinois had said, the blue eyeshadow gave a mysterious quality to her warm brown eyes.

The slate blue sundress with white jacket always brought her compliments. She stepped into white pumps and fastened pearl earrings to match the single strand around her neck. Staring at the reflection, she knew everything looked right, and yet it was all surface. There was no inner glow. How could there be? Her time in the Philippines was almost over. Soon, she would be leaving behind a man and a little boy that she had grown to love.

Almost without thinking, she applied perfume, as if it made a difference.

Eric met them almost as soon as she, John and Maureen arrived inside the front entrance. "Come!" he said, excitement in his voice. "You must see Orlando. He was moved out of intensive care into a private room this morning."

They hurried with Eric to the room. He stopped outside the door. "Maila is with him. She wants to see you first, Stacey. Then John and Maureen can go in for a moment."

Slowly, Stacey opened the door and quietly slipped inside. Maila sat beside the bed, holding Orlando's hand. His eyes were closed and his face appeared gaunt beneath the thick bandage circling his head.

Maila carefully moved her hand away from Orlando's, then came over to Stacey, standing near the door. "Stacey, Eric doesn't love me. He told Orlando he loves me like a daughter. Orlando . . ." She looked over her shoulder toward him, then back at Stacey, her eyes glowing with warm moisture, "Orlando still loves me. He wants to marry me."

"Is that what you want, Maila?"

She nodded. "More than anything in the world."

Stacey embraced her friend.

"He's very weak," Maila said, moving back to the bed, but there's no fever now. He can talk a little. It's all right if you want to speak to him. The others may come in, too."

"I've seen him several times today," Eric said when Stacey opened the door. Maureen and John went over to speak briefly with Orlando, then left. When Stacey touched his arm, his eyes weakly met her own. She could barely hear his raspy whisper.

"You know?" he asked, looking toward Maila.

Stacey nodded. "I'm glad for you both, Orlando." He started to speak again. She held up a restraining hand. "Save your strength, Orlando. You must hurry and get well."

Although faint, the curve of his lips formed a smile. The first one she had ever seen, "We'll talk soon," she told Maila, and left the room.

John and Maureen excused themselves, explaining they had a few others to visit, and Eric offered to take Stacey back to the apartment.

"Is that all right with you Stacey?" he asked.

After visiting with Fredrico for a few minutes, the blue Lincoln sped along the moonlit streets of Manila. Eric did not head for the apartment, but stopped near the Luneta esplanade.

They walked along the esplanade and into the nearby park. "It's quite safe," Eric explained as they entered the fragrant, tree-lined park with its many couples strolling between well-lighted rows of shrubs and flowers. Others stood close beneath trees, out of the path of searching moonbeams.

Eric led her to a bench beneath a palm. He leaned back against the seat, stretched his legs out in front, crossing them at the ankles, and propped his hands behind his head. After inhaling deeply and exhaling he said, "It's good to sit and relax for a change, isn't it, Stacey?"

"I suppose so," she replied shortly, feeling indignant that he would bring her to such a place, where lovers passed hand in hand, talking intimately, laughing softly.

Then he sat up straight and turned to her. "You're not relaxing, Stacey." She sat stiffly, her hands clasped demurely on her lap. "In fact, you're being quite distant." She turned her head away, but his fingers brought it back. "Tell me, about it," he said.

"I'm just concerned about Fredrico." Her questioning eyes met his. "Why don't you want me to adopt him, Eric?"

When he didn't reply, she felt defensive. "I realize I know very little about rearing a child. But, Eric, many of my friends have children several years old. They've learned as they go along. Any my parents would help. Fredrico is not the typical child. He knows that God has a special purpose in his life. He needs someone who understands that. His potential is astounding."

"I realize all that, Stacey." Eric shifted on the bench and stretched his arm along the back. "Maureen's telling me your plans just took me by surprise. I should have known, but so much has been on my mind. I too, have been thinking about the boy's future."

He touched her shoulder with his fingers, his eyes thoughtfully watching the movement. "So much is uncertain at the moment," he said, looking at her face again. "After my transfer to the States comes through, I'll have a command post there, then perhaps after retirement, I'll teach at Annapolis. Where I will be is not definite. But I was thinking about taking Fredrico with me. And, of course, adoption would be necessary."

"Oh, Eric," Stacey said apologetically. "I didn't mean to interfere. It's just that I love him so and want to help. Family life, mothering, would be good for him. But more important, he needs opportunity. You can provide that easier than I," she sighed.

"No," he said emphatically. "I still think it's too big a job for a single parent."

Stacey closed her eyes against the impossible thought that formed in her mind. She wouldn't allow it. "You think neither of us should adopt him, then?" she asked, trying to ignore the disconcerting movement of his fingers on her shoulder.

"It's something that needs careful thought," he replied seriously. "In fact," he added quickly. "There are several things we have to discuss."

"Like what?" she asked.

"We have a wedding to plan for our foster daughter."

Stacey smiled. "I'll do what I can. But I don't expect they'll want a big one. Or to wait long."

Eric looked out thoughtfully, his eyes resting momentarily on a passing couple. "It took a while for me to piece it all together. After I questioned Tomas, he confessed Orlando's love for Maila. It seems they've waited a long time already. It's almost unbelievable they would sacrifice themselves like that." He glanced at her. "For me!" he added.

"They're remarkable people," she said.

Eric agreed. "Yes, and I'm beginning to understand what a really fine man Orlando is. Maila has always been special to me. I suppose that's why I was so blind to the situation. Then after you told me she loved me, I didn't know how to go about letting her know she was like a daughter to me, without harming our relationship."

"But it worked out beautifully," Stacey said quietly.

"Now it's time to settle things between us, Stacey," he said softly, moving closer, his arm circled her shoulders.

She caught her breath and looked into his eyes, watching the strange tricks the moonlight played there.

"What do you mean?" she asked breathlessly, as his other hand reached her neck and the fingers were moving to the back of her head.

"I mean," he said, bending closer. "You and I have some unfinished business."

"Like . . . like what?"

"Like this," he said. His lips touched her cheeks. "You're remarkably beautiful tonight." And her lips. "I love you, Stacey," he breathed against them.

Then he moved back just enough to see her face. She knew it was unnecessary to say anything. There was no preventing the spread of her lips into a smile, nor to keep the feeling from her eyes, or to stop her arms from reaching up to draw him closer.

"I love you, Eric. So much, I can hardly believe it."

Then he kissed her thoroughly, stopping only long enough to ask, "Then you'll marry me?"

"Oh, yes, Eric. I want that so much."

Moving away reluctantly, he asked, "What kind of wedding do you want?"

She told him about the elaborate church wedding she had always envisioned. The many bridesmaids. The lovely gown. The huge reception at the college. "That was a beautiful dream, Eric. But it's not so important. It's a marriage I want. With the man I love."

"Why not both?" he questioned, his cheeks dimpling. "Suppose you return to Illinois, plan the kind of wedding you want. I'll stay here, sell the farm, and see what we can do about Fredrico. I think it will be good to put a little distance between you and Fredrico to ensure your decision is not just an emotional one."

She knew he was right. "My father suggested that." She sighed deeply. "But it saddens me to think I have so little time left here. And that I would leave here without you and Fredrico. It would be so final."

"Stacey," he said softly, lifting her chin with his fingers. "There was one thing I wasn't entirely truthful about. What I implied about not pursuing you." He shook his head. "You can't get away from me now. Wherever you go, I'll be there. And you'll see. The time will pass quickly."

It passed all too quickly. Maila and Orlando wanted only a small ceremony in the hospital chapel, with Stacey as the only bridesmaid. It was decided they would wait until after Orlando's complete recuperation before having a big reception at the villa. Eric said their wedding present would be a trip to America. That way, Maila could come to the wedding as Stacey's matron of honor.

John said nothing could stop him from being best man and Maureen offered to pour the punch. Fredrico's bravery, in spite of her own tears, touched her heart when they said goodbye. She realized it best not to tell him about a possible adoption just yet. He needed time and space for his own adjustments and acceptance. But she knew she wouldn't change her mind about wanting him for her own little boy.

When the plane left her loved ones behind, a loneliness settled in. But they would always be in her heart.

Two months later, Stacey dressed in her bone-colored suit and rust-colored blouse, the outfit she had worn on her arrival in the Philippines. She got into her car in Carbondale and drove to the airport. The time had fled, but the phone bills were enormous. Wedding plans and parties had been exciting. But no feeling could compare with the mixture of anxiety and elation she felt waiting for the plane.

It arrived. On time. Then she saw the two most important men in her life. Fredrico wore a blue suit and a tie. He carried the ukelele. Then he saw her and began to run. She knelt down to hug him tightly.

Then she lifted her eyes to the handsome commander in a white uniform. She saw the blue of the sky in his eyes, and the warmth of a summer's day in his smile.

She stood, then fell into his open arms that enfolded her against his chest. "My darling," he said as his lips touched hers. Now she knew how foolish she was to have feared the summer's end in the Philippines. She had so much more. A wonderful man loved her. And their hearts, now beating as one, offered each other a lifetime of love.

ABOUT THE AUTHOR

Yvonne Lehman is a wife, mother of four, and novelist living in Black Mountain, located in the panoramic Blue Ridge Mountains of western North Carolina. For articles, short stories, and books, she has received awards from *Decision Magazine* (Dwight L. Moody Award for Excellence in Writing), National League of American Pen Women, Writer's Digest, and New York Romantic Times Booklovers Conference (Inspirational Award). She is author of two mainstream novels, one historical, and four inspirational romances. Two of her novels have been published in Holland and Germany.

Her Bachelor's Degree is from the University of North Carolina, Asheville, and her Master's Degree in English is from Western Carolina University. She teaches English and Creative Writing at a community college. Yvonne is founder and director of the Blue Ridge Writers Conference.

Forever Romances are inspirational romances designed to bring you a joyful, heart-lifting reading experience. If you would like more information about joining our Forever Romance book series, please write to us:

Guideposts Customer Service
39 Seminary Hill Road
Carmel, NY 10512

Forever Romances are chosen by the same staff that prepares *Guideposts,* a monthly magazine filled with true stories of people's adventures in faith. *Guideposts* is not sold on the newsstand. It's available by subscription only. And subscribing is easy. Write to the address above and you can begin reading *Guideposts* soon. When you subscribe, each month you can count on receiving exciting new evidence of God's Presence, His Guidance and His limitless love for all of us.